COAST-TO-COAST ACCLAIM FOR FABIENNE MARSH'S

LONG DISTANCES

"What an impressive debut. . . . Great charm and power and the ability to breathe life into each character. *LONG DISTANCES* deserves every hyperbole it receives. The reviewer would attempt to add an ornate and spectacular one here, but he is too impatient to get back and re-read the book."

—*Orange County Register* (California)

"Fabienne Marsh uses a respected literary form, the epistolary, seldom seen in contemporary works, with skill, grace and deft effectiveness; she creates a real and likeable family. . . ."

—*Pittsburgh Press*

"A skillful novel that has much to say about the hazards of modern marriage, conflicting ambitions and the risk of abandoning a safe, stay-at-home life to chase a dream. . . ."

—*Virginian-Pilot/Ledger-Star*

"Marsh concentrates a wealth of information about her characters—details of emotion, particularly—in not much space. . . . She makes Michael and Kate seem so real. . . . *LONG DISTANCES* has a provocative energy."

—*People*

"A fresh spin on (the) first novel. . . ."

—*The New York Times Book Review*

"A surprisingly accomplished and unusual effort for a first-time author. . . ."

—*ALA Booklist*

"A SUPERB FEAT OF MAGIC, A MASTERFUL NOVEL."

—*San Mateo Times* (California)

LONG DISTANCES

FABIENNE MARSH

WASHINGTON SQUARE PRESS
PUBLISHED BY POCKET BOOKS
New York London Toronto Sydney Tokyo

We have made every effort to trace the ownership of all copyrighted material and to secure permission from copyright holders. In the event of any question arising as to the use of any material, we will be pleased to make the necessary corrections in future printings. Thanks are due to the following authors, publishers, publications, and agents for permission to use the material indicated.

Excerpt from "Four for Sir John Davies." Copyright 1953 by Theodore Roethke from *The Collected Poems of Theodore Roethke*. Reprinted by permission of Doubleday, a division of Bantam, Doubleday, Dell Publishing Group, Inc.

From *Midpoint and Other Poems* by John Updike. Copyright © 1969 by John Updike. Reprinted by permission of Alfred A. Knopf, Inc.

Ezra Pound, *Personae*. Copyright 1926 by Ezra Pound. Reprinted by permission of New Directions Publishing Corporation.

Excerpt from "Undine" from *Poems 1965–1975*. © 1966, 1969, 1972, 1975, 1980 by Seamus Heaney. Reprinted by permission of Farrar, Straus and Giroux, Inc. Excerpt from *A View from the Chorus* by Abram Tertz (Andre Sinyavsky) English translation copyright © 1976 by William Collins Sons & Co. Ltd. Reprinted by permission of Farrar, Straus and Giroux, Inc.

Thomas Wolfe, excerpted from *Look Homeward, Angel.* Copyright 1929 Charles Scribners Sons; copyright renewed © 1957 Edward C. Aswell, administrator, C.T.A. and/or Fred W. Wolfe. Reprinted with the permission of Charles Scribners Sons, an imprint of Macmillan Publishing Company.

A Washington Square Press Publication of
POCKET BOOKS, a division of Simon & Schuster Inc.
1230 Avenue of the Americas, New York, NY 10020

Library of Congress Catalog Card Number: 87-19438

ISBN: 0-671-67400-5

First Washington Square Press printing March 1989

10 9 8 7 6 5 4 3 2 1

Printed in the U.S.A.

Contents

Part One

LONDON

Michaelmas

I often sit down to a letter not because I intend writing
anything of importance to you, but just to touch
a piece of paper which you will be holding in your hand.

Sinyavsky

Le péché est la chose qu'on ne peut pas ne pas faire.

Gide

Inwood Road
Pleasantville, New York

September 17, 1982

Dearest Michael,

Today Judson sucked so hard on a Dixie cup his mouth turned purple. At first I thought he had come back from his trumpet lesson, where bee-stung lips are the sign of a good hour's work. No such luck. Scrunch, who had witnessed the horror, informed me (sobbing all the while) that Judson had been demonstrating what Mr. Fishman, his fourth-grade science teacher, had taught him about suction: "Judson made a vacuum and when he let go ten minutes later it was purple underneath." Dr. Nelson said Judson popped all his blood vessels and told him it would take two weeks for the clown mouth to go away. No sooner had those words been spoken than *my* mouth took a turn for the worse, distorting itself with remarks I had, until that moment, withheld from your son, who, for good measure, smashed Stu Bush in class again.

I miss you and give you a white-hot kiss.

Kate

P.S. Judson feels he has been punished unjustly and encloses his Magna Charta.

Inwood Road
Pleasantville, New York

September 17, 1982

Dad—

I'm punished because I tried to teach Scrunch about sukshun. Also I hit Stu in class because he hit me from behind with a rubberband. *But he stopped bleeding*. Mom took the television downstairs but Scrunch and I carried it back up while Mom was at work. Mom said SHIT when she came home. How come *she* never gets punished?

Love, Judson

Somewhere over the Atlantic

10:35 PM

Dearest Kate,

I'm in a bit of a whiskey haze (only two). I'm trying to sleep off the departure scene at the airport, but every time I close my eyes, I see *yours*, sea-green, stormy, and hurt. And I feel like a dog.

Our ancient wish to spend a year in England ripens for me, not for you. I had hoped, as much as you, the film on Northern Ireland would get you over here. Uprooting Judson and Jeanne might have been difficult, but, even then, we'd have worked it out.

I want you to believe all this, rather than simply accept my departure. At the same time, I know that, believe what you will, my sabbatical places a very great burden on you. So, here I am, at 30,000 feet, experiencing an extremely self-conscious weightlessness: leaving you and the children was not the plan—even if something about this third book demands a new landscape.

Jack Daniels has been speaking with little discipline, but with greater truth than you know.

Flight. Turbulence outside and, beamed at my temple, a miniature gale from the nozzle controlling the air conditioning. All six feet of me are folded between Clara, a kind, religious woman, who crosses herself repeatedly, and Martin, a British commodities trader (mostly zinc), who is quietly scraping off the beef (probably Wellington) that has landed on his trousers.

I'm not hungry. And I keep hoping my heartless pillow, no bigger than a lozenge, will turn into your luscious shoulder. Already it's disorienting to wake up without you—that feeling at waking of not belonging anywhere.

I'm rambling, but I love you.

Michael

32 Cleveland Square
London W2
(Miss Holliday's room gets three stars.)

September 29, 1982

Dearest K–

That rotten Stu Bush got what he deserved. Don't tell Judson that, but *do* tell him to lead with his left. As for Jeanne ("but you can call me Scrunch"), sounds like the usual prepuberty exuberance. Last spring she plucked our mountain laurels clean and, thanks to their sticky stems, made herself a fresh pair of earrings every day. And remember her unladylike habit of sitting on sprinklers to stop the jet?

~~You've stirred at least two~~ This was about to be a claim that you'd set off a string of new poems in me, which gives you some indication that my book is coming along. And since you've started that old stunt—I think you're the ~~most extraordinary woman I have ever met~~ and I ~~think about you~~ *at least* three times a day.

All my love,
Michael

Inwood Road
Pleasantville, New York

October 2, 1982

Dearest Michael,

Your colleague from the Philosophy Department is after me again. I dropped by Lewisohn to pick up your mail and bumped into Bill, who was on his way to the Nietzsche "Life Without God" seminar he's offering this term. He asked if you liked London and gave me the name of a friend of his who teaches in the International Relations Department at The London School of Economics—Susan Fleet. He wants you to look her up. After that, he told me I never should have switched majors from Philosophy to English, even if I had gotten an English professor along with the degree. Hard for me to believe that, fourteen years later, he even thinks about all this. Anyway, I rushed back to work to look at footage that had come in from El Salvador. One crazy French cameraman, a war junkie, told me last August that he could supply the network with all the battle footage we needed from Central America. So far he has. I'm waiting for them to approve my proposal—if they do I'll have to do some of the location work.

Miss you terribly. Thank Jack Daniels for me; he elicited a rare confession from you. I wish the timing had been better for getting us all to London. Sometimes I worry that we've fallen out of phase—but it *is* only a year.

xxK.

Cleveland Square
London W2

October 16, 1982

Dearest K–

There I was on the Central Line. The doors opened at Tottenham Court Road, revealing all the bright Italian tiles that were being installed. And all of a sudden I thought of Scrunch buffing *our* linoleum tiles, the buffer stronger than she, overtaking her toes with coarse whiskers that made her hopscotch and cry, "YOUCH!" Don't know what possessed me, but I could not suppress a smile, first, then a laugh–full throttle. Of course, no one noticed. Or rather, *everyone* did but pretended not to. Only the hand grips–a row of plastic balls bobbing on their coils–seemed to ratify my mood. This is a long way of saying I miss you all very much.

Miss Holliday checks up on me regularly and charges me a modest 35 pounds per week (finances will be a stretch; if a *strain*, I'll hammer out reviews) for a small white room with a 12-foot ceiling and an enormous window that overlooks the square. I run into her when we collect our mail at 8 AM and, once again, at 12 noon. For the second mail drop, Miss Holliday comes down in a leotard and skirt. "I'm off to my Keep Fit class," she says on her way to Porchester Hall. She is 76.

On the subject of longevity, I thought we had agreed, heart-throb, that your war-zone days were over. Have them send one of the many young, ambitious vacuums I met at that Christmas party you dragged me to (the one your boss gave in honor of the employees she had just fired). And stay away from Bill. Just like him to muscle in on my woman while I'm gone. What will he do when he runs out of former students to date? Don't feel like giving Ms. Fleet a ring, either.

M.

P.S. Everything they say about the weather is true!

HOTEL HONDURAS

Dominating the Skyline of Tegucigalpa, designed and built for your ultimate comfort. Located in a residential area a few blocks from the center of town.

10/23/82

Amor—Hotter than *Inferno*, Canto XIV, down here. Military advisors (U.S. and Argentine), U.N. relief workers, diplomats and journalists coexist around the best pool (see verso) in this parched country.

Some are waiting to go to El Salvador, a few will go to Nicaragua, and I need to go to both countries. (They've given me the go-ahead for a documentary on Central America.) I return on the 30th.

Mom has the children.

Te quiero, K.

Correo
Aereo

POST CARD
ADDRESS

Señor Michael Hammond
32 Cleveland Square
Flat 8
London W2, England

INGLATERRA

COLUMBIA UNIVERSITY

Philosophy Hall

October 25, 1982

Dear Kate.

Enjoyed our brief encounter a few weeks ago, even if it did serve to remind me that poets get all the girls.

I've been reading Eileen Simpson's book, *Poets in Their Youth,* and find myself wholly absorbed. She was John Berryman's first wife, and fondly recalls him (an alcoholic suicide), R. P. Blackmur (both he and his wife alcoholics), Robert Lowell (certified manic depressive), Delmore Schwartz (alcoholic paranoid), Randall Jarrell (almost normal), and Allen Tate (womanizer). Tate was the oldest and outlived the rest, which shows that fucking is healthier than drinking.

Give me a call if you're lonely. Don't know why Michael chose to spend his sabbatical year in England to finish the book. Distance erodes relationships.

Semper Fidelis,
Bill

32 Cleveland Square
London W2

October 26, 1982

Dearest Kate,

Westminster *is not* Westminister; and Tottenham *is* Tottnum—at every opportunity, they saw off syllables and swallow vowels . . . except for băsil, bāsil and bAHsil. Had to ask for all three before I got what I wanted the other day. When it came to any TAYtoe or TAHtoe products, my American was irrepressible.

Are my little Yanks well?

Was scribbling near the Serpentine today, then took a walk and came across the changing of the guard—a magnificent trail of red and black that was greeted by the traffic near Marble Arch with as much enthusiasm as a Union Pacific freight train in the deep South.

Love, M.

Inwood Road
Pleasantville, New York

Saturday, October 31, 1982

Dearest Michael,

Elaine stopped by today. Dr. Nelson told her you were on sabbatical and she wanted to see how I was holding up. Her divorce is about to come through and she has won custody of the children. She thought it hideous of you (you know how direct she can be) to leave me for the year and, in the same breath, tried to sell me one of those home-exercise mini-trampolines (no thanks). I told her the kids continued to enjoy the *World Book* she had sold us and qualified my praise by telling her that the picture of the lamprey should be removed from the "L" volume because it had given Scrunch nightmares. Nobody wants encyclopedias anymore, she said, then very sweetly offered to take the kids if I ever wanted to work, get away, or fly over to see you.

As she was about to leave, she stopped and asked if I would mind reading the personal she was going to put in *New York* magazine:

> Lithe, lovely, 38-year-old mother of two
> seeks responsible, intelligent professional
> with warm sense of humor. Must love children.

Doesn't seem fair that she has to go through this crap, but I hope it works. I told her I was confident she would haul in a nice Jewish guy. You mean a boring orthodontist, shc said.

I feel so lucky having you.

Love, Kate

P.S. For Halloween, will you be handing out McVities Plain Chocolate Digestives or, God forbid, Scotch eggs? Elaine made us taste the pumpkin tortellini from Bologna they were featuring at Food Fair this week. What those Italian pasta makers must think of us!

Inwood Road
Pleasantville, New York

October 31, 1982

Dear Dad,

At Grand Union the check-out ladies wore witches hats and black capes. I'm too old to dress up this year (don't forget my birthday on November 24), but I'll wrap the UNICEF money in foil and give out the Milky Ways if Mom doesn't eat them all. Judson wants to be a boxer.

Are your poems done yet?

Love, Scrunch

Inwood Road
Pleasantville, New York

October 31, 1982

Dad–

I borrowed Joey's boxing gloves and Everready shorts. Mom says I'll be cold and is trying to cover me up. I wish you were here.

Joey's Dad is on Hollywood Squares. So Joey will either dress up as an X or O.

Hurry up with your book!!!

Love, Judson

Inwood Road
Pleasantville, New York

Sunday, November 1, 1982

Darling—

You needn't have worried about my safety last week, but I'm glad you called today all the same. Seems you barely had time to clear your throat before that pound-hungry coin box *pip-pip*'ed for more. Don't they have engineers over there? Sorry, but the static reminded me of my grandfather's RCA Victrola. And how much extra do they charge us for the echo chamber?

Ah, but to hear that steady voice of yours, *pianissimo ma non troppo!* You must have melted every female cable in the Atlantic.

On weekends I miss you most.

K.

Cleveland Square
London W2

Sunday, November 1

Dearest Kate,

For the better part of an hour, I've been staring at a picture of you. Your green eyes are even bigger than I remember. And that mane of yours, its color rich as loam.

I find myself missing all of you and, only now, understand that pig, Goethe, counting hexameters on his lover's back!

Sometimes I think I must be mad to leave my wife and children for a monk's room in a genteel city best suited for writers or convalescents.*

I miss you.

Michael

* . . . or English professors. Good news in your last Columbia mail drop. Peter Clare will be here with Cathy for six months' research in Oxford. Don't know how he got the time off, but I look forward to having him here.

DR. WALTER FEINSTEIN
30 Rockefeller Plaza
New York, New York, 10020

November 3, 1982

Dear Kate,

Our records show that it has been over 6 months since your last prophylactic treatment.

Please call our office to make an appointment.

Walter Feinstein, D.D.S.

Kate Hammond
12 Inwood Road
Pleasantville, New York
10570

Cleveland Square
London W2

November 5, 1982

Dearest K–

This time I was on the Jubilee Line. Destination: The Poetry Library at 105 Piccadilly. The doors opened and I read the following:

HOW WE DIVERTED THE
NORTH SEA MUSSELS FROM THEIR
LOVE MAKING ACTIVITIES

Underneath these words, the photograph of a single mussel—barnacled, battered, suffering a sea change, not to mention a sex change– all brought about by Shell Oil. And why? Because the poor bastard had clung to Shell's lovely, leggy sea platforms, as well as clustered promiscuously. *"This is why we at Shell developed Aquatect: a special rubbery coating which prevents mussels and other marine life from clinging to future underwater structures. Making sure that whenever a large wave arrives, the mussels will float off in search of a more comfortable home. One where we won't interfere with their personal habits."*

What I want to know is this. How's a man (or woman) supposed to go to work without being provoked into thinking about Man (or Woman) as Mussel. I feel for that mussel, or rather, I know exactly how that mussel feels—adrift and looking for a cluster.

I reeled off a couple of blockbusting stanzas—"The North Sea Mussel," a massive modern poem—

then despised and shelved it. My other stuff (I think) holds more promise.

Please, intrepid one, beware of countries ending in *-dor* and *-agua;* if nothing else, won't you tire of eating things that finish with *-ito?* I'd prefer, even, your *second* proposal, the one on toxic water mentioned on the phone. Have they approved it?

Pumpkin tortellini feels a long way away. There's no trick-or-treat here. They just bob for apples and discuss witches. Now that you've finished with Halloween, I suppose you'll be gearing up for Thanksgiving. Then Christmas!

Shall we show the children London this December, or shall I come home?

xx to you and JudScrunch

Inwood Road
Pleasantville, New York

November 15, 1982

Dear Walter,

Prophylactic treatment?! Until I saw the D.D.S., I worried about my Southern Hemisphere. And what a shocking note to send by postcard, for all to see! Not everyone shares your definition of prophylactics.

Sec you in January.

Kate Hammond

Inwood Road
Pleasantville, New York

November 15, 1982

M—

You are not and never will be a mussel. If you are "adrift and looking for a cluster," you have only to come home—you know, Platform 12, Inwood Road.

And goddamn it, take *cabs* if every journey in the tube causes these existential epiphanies.

I'm volcanic today because, again, when I was picking up your mail I bumped into Nietzsche. And *that* would have been fine, had Mom not been with me. After a brief chat on the subject of Cardinal John Henry Newman, who, we were told, was the most brilliant cleric of the nineteenth century and who, early on, recognized the threat of rationalistic secularism, Mom ("I've always liked Bill") invited him to Thanksgiving dinner. Brilliant. I can just hear Bill and Elaine, whom I've also invited, discussing his favorite book,* Kundera's *The Incredible Lightness of Being:* Elaine—"Is it a diet book?"; Bill—"Well, compared to Hegel's *Phenomenology of the Mind,* yes."

To make matters worse, they've decided to axe my documentary on Central America. No interest, they say (no *ratings,* they mean). So there you have it—months of research for nothing.

And only because you brought up Aquatect, Shell Oil's contribution to prophylactic research, will I enclose a copy of the postcard I received from my dentist. I might add that when I went to Dr. Casey yesterday, the doctor who *really* handles these things, she asked if everything was okay between us. Why, I asked. Well, she said, poking my trampoline (as you call it) for a routine inspection. Seems this diaphragm has not been used in a while. It's lost its elasticity. Well, I said, my husband's in London for the year. Oh, she said.

Come home for Christmas.

K.

P.S. Bill asked if you had looked up his friend.

* What have you been reading?

Moorland Drive
Pleasantville, New York

November 16, 1982

Dear Kate,

I know I'm just a few doors down but, after a lousy marriage, I'm trying to do things properly—so I thought I'd accept your gracious Thanksgiving invitation by writing rather than calling.

Things are going well for the kids. Josh got the lead in the fifth grade play. He's playing Ben Franklin, which accounts for his behavior around the neighborhood—keys and kites, and that soprano solo, "Half the Battle." Terry was elected to Safety Patrol. I don't know how they convince these kids that it's a great honor. As far as I can tell, the only difference it has made in her life is that she has to get up an hour earlier to put her white belt and badge on and stand at the traffic crossing at the entrance to the school parking lot. Under normal circumstances, I cannot get her out of bed.

I've had 238 responses to my ad in *New York* magazine. 200 were form letters. 25 were from men who should have had enough sense *not* to enclose a picture. 5 were Scientologists. I've dated the remaining 8 and enclose a copy of the list I use to keep them straight:

	Name	*Position*	*Description*	*Comments*
1.	Harold Kapinsky 51, Single	Accountant	5′8″, bald with braces (bridgework), pudgy.	Repulsive.

2. Sheldon Nelson 38, Single	Broker	5′8″, curly black hair, works out.	Nice teeth, but chews with his mouth open.
3. Jefferson Dean 35, Single	Baptist Minister	6′0″, blond, blue eyes, in shape.	A God. But tried to convert me on the first date.
4. Keldon Steele 54, Divorced	Banker	Banker suit, blond, 5′10″.	Absolutely nothing in common.
5. Patrick Gifford 48, Divorced	Banker	Banker suit, blond, 5′8″.	Has 4 kids, kind.
6. David Greenfield 49, Divorced	Advertising Executive	5′9″, curly gray hair, plays squash.	Has 2 kids, cute.
7. James Stone 35, Divorced	Newspaper Editor	5′11″, brown hair, glasses, thin.	Drank 2 bottles of wine. Chain smoker.
8. Jack Feldman 35, Single	Account Manager	5′5″, brown hair.	Plays bass guitar, funny.

Gifford, Greenfield, and Feldman are contenders. You would not believe how much crap there is out there.

See you on Thanksgiving. I'll make the pumpkin pie.

Love, Elaine

Inwood Road
Pleasantville, New York

November 17, 1982

Dearest Michael,

It's 2 AM. I've just awakened from a horrible dream—no: *worse* than horrible since you're not here.

A Maryknoll relief worker came to my tent in the middle of the night to tell me that refugees would be crossing the Honduran border at dawn. I woke the crew up, told them to put on their flak jackets, and asked them to meet me in an hour by the infirmary. From there, we hiked to a river some 3 kilometers away. We arrived in time to see U.S. helicopters churning up the river with gunfire, hitting 4 of the 20 or so peasants, one of them a woman whose child had Judson's eyes. The child was within reach; the mother had been hit, and was struggling with a bundle of possessions which seemed to be dragging her downstream. I grabbed the child, was reassured to see the mother regain her footing—she *hadn't* been hit! When I got to the river bank, I realized *it was the child who had been hit.* Blood from the little body was streaming down my clothes. I couldn't stop *SCREAMING!* The next thing I knew, Judson was hugging me, telling me to wake up.

Michael, I just don't seem to be able to *leave* these very sad places. I don't want these assignments. I don't want these dreams. I don't want to dream them without you.

Love, Kate

Cleveland Square
London W2

November 17, 1982

Dear Jeanne,

Eleven years old! A very serious age. Mother tells me you have expressed an interest in pantyhose, especially these— : I'm afraid they'll have to be approved by her. Until then, I enclose the most interesting socks I could find. The warmest ones look as if they're part animal, part sock—thick as a horse's coat in winter. When you come to London, I'll take you to the zoo in Regent's Park, where you can see what a British jaguar looks like, and how he behaves.

I hope you have not outgrown these things. When I was eleven, I wanted to be the engineer who pulled the whistle on the train that cut through our backyard. The following year, I wanted to be the conductor of a symphony orchestra; when I saw my first performance on television, I thought all the music was coming out of his baton! What do you want to be?

For your birthday, will you take your friends bowling, skating, or something else this year?

I miss you and think about you, Judson, and Mommy a great deal.

Love, Daddy

Cleveland Square
London W2

November 23, 1982

Dearest K–

I've just received your letter. I wish I had been beside you when you dreamed that speechless horror.

And I'm angry they buried your show. I'm not sure I understand network thinking—this time or ever. The whole damn business is poison, the way they toy with people's lives. *Rotten* business—run, now, by a niggardly bunch of actuaries. Can only get worse.

I hope you'll soon be showing me that Water is no longer as simple as 2-parts Hydrogen to 1-part Oxygen. I would worry less.

(And, speaking of worry, I am *not* relieved by your mother's invitation to William the Conquerer for Thanksgiving dinner.)

Nothing else, except that I want to say, and can never say enough, that I *know* how hard I'm making it for you and the children this year. We discussed this, but I think it's worth repeating: I really need this time away to make these poems work and, whatever the consequences, *that* much is being accomplished. I've managed to uncover old subjects and renew them here. But I could have done all this, probably better, if you and the children had come. I'm lonelier than I expected to be and, to give you a sense of just how lonely—I'm meeting Susan Fleet for lunch next week at a coffeeshop on Kingsway, near The London School of Economics (LSE).

For poetry, I'm reading Hopkins (always), Heaney and Osip Mandelstam*; in fiction, Ford Madox Ford's *The Good Soldier* (a very bible of Catholic sexual jealousy) and Kipling (cracking stories with no women in).

I love you.

M.

* Plus the bilge I've been writing.

Inwood Road
Pleasantville, New York

November 25, 1982

Dear Michael,

I have been getting letter after letter from an unsympathetic sender in Wilmington, Delaware. The zip code has nine places, not counting the hyphen, and they've just started using red ink and BOLD TYPE.

For God's sake (and mine), why don't you have your mail forwarded? Today, I finally opened one of the barking envelopes:

ACCOUNT CLOSED. RETURN YOUR CARDS, CUT IN HALF, IF YOU HAVE NOT ALREADY DONE SO.
TOTAL FINANCE CHARGE DUE IMMEDIATELY: $653.00

They threaten to get the balance with the help of a collection agency. I enclose the rest of their correspondence.

Hope it's not too late for you, jailbird.

XX Kate

P.S. Saw Peter up at Columbia—says he can't wait to see you!

THE CUMBERLAND GAP
The historic Cumberland Gap borders three states: Kentucky, Tennessee and West Virginia.

Air Mail

12/1/82

Hon –

In most hotels, you can crack the spine when you open the Gideon bible. Here in Kentucky it is well-thumbed, spongy, and the loudest voice in the room – discounting an overactive heater. This county's dry, but Cainer, my source on cruddy water down here, smuggled in moonshine (to counteract any toxic chemicals, you understand).

Mom behaved on Thanksgiving and spoke with your brother as well as with Bill. Very pleasant. 22 days until I'm in your arms! K.

Mister Michael Hammond
32 Cleveland Square
Flat 8
London W2
ENGLAND

A HOPELESS DAWN 1888
Frank Bramley
Oil on canvas 122.6 × 168.6 cm/48¼ × 66 in.
Tate Gallery (1627)

(Just sent that damn finance charge to Wilmington, Delaware.)

12/4/82

Dearest K—

Bad news* in that last pack of mail you forwarded to me: my publisher's gone bust. My editor assures me that Hunter, Stein in the U.S. and Queen's Press here will pick up the manuscript.

TWA Flight No. 402, arriving at 4 PM on 12/22

Love,
M.

*Won't let it ruin our time together.

Air Mail

Kate Hammond
12 Inwood Road
Pleasantville, New York
10570
U.S.A.

Inwood Road
Pleasantville, New York

December 6, 1982

Dearest Michael,

In an attempt to get close to you, I put aside any literature on carbon filtration or solvents in drinking water (mostly trichloroethylene and carbon tetrachloride) and picked up *The Good Soldier*. Got three-quarters of the way through and stopped. Nothing to do with Catholic jealousy (forgive me)—characters too Waspy for *that;* they left me COLD.

But what do *I* know? Only that I wish the fellow reading the book were here with me right now.

K.

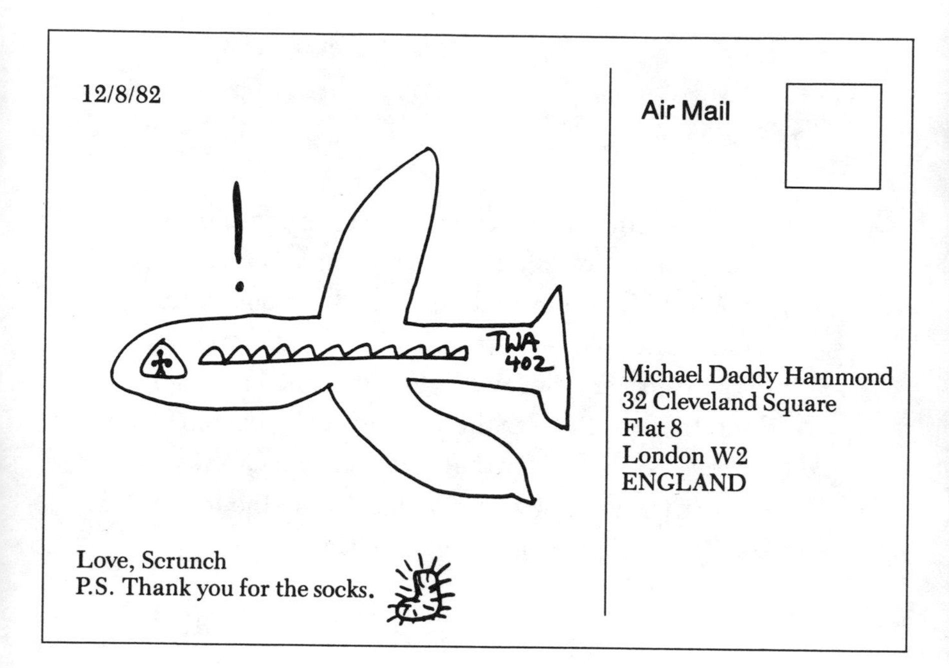
12/8/82

Air Mail

TWA 402

Michael Daddy Hammond
32 Cleveland Square
Flat 8
London W2
ENGLAND

Love, Scrunch
P.S. Thank you for the socks.

Cleveland Square
London W2

December 10, 1982

Dearest K–

I awoke to the sound of a diminished chord at 8 AM and realized that the City of Westminster garbage truck had made my Timex travel alarm obsolete.

Had some tea, toast (with Miss Holliday's cherry jam), choked on a pit, revived; wrote a bit (could not summon any electrons), and set off for The London School of Economics, where, after numerous cancellations, Susan Fleet and I were to meet.

Took the Central Line and got off at Holbourn, which, next to the one in Moscow, has the longest escalator I have ever ridden. Stopped by Sir John Soane's Museum in Lincoln's Inn Fields, then on to the day's worth of lectures Ms. Fleet said I might enjoy, had I nothing better to do. I had not.

Darling, I know you think *I* teach in a dump—but only because you have not seen the LSE. A cement mixer stood in front of the administration building. Sawdust, paint, wood, and concrete made the halls an obstacle course. A cardboard sign at the entrance to the East Building advertised COFFEE and, after a terrifying ride in an elevator with no doors, I found the little dungeon. Only a Thesean sense got me out of the enormously complicated building.

What the school lacks in beauty, it makes up for in brains—which brings me to my lecture summary:

International History—Professor MacSomething said Charles VIII of France was a half-wit who had freed himself of a bossy sister and, intending to start a new Crusade against Constantinople, actually *had* the robes made for his anticipated coronation as Holy Roman Emperor! All plans foiled when, in 1498, Charles hit his head on the lintel of a low doorway and died of apoplexy.

Mac then accused French troops of bringing syphilis to Italy and slimed the entire Valois family, insisting that, by the mid-sixteenth century, ONE-THIRD of Paris had contracted the dreaded disease (*encore une perfidie Anglaise*).

International Relations—Professor Aitken would not start the lecture until the American in the front row had gotten rid of her Kit-Kat and coffee. "At the LSE, we discourage this North American practice of eating in class." I'll have to try that line on Columbia students—HA! He then lectured on the Korean War as a case study in Crisis Decision-making.

Political Economy—Professor Fleet lectured on Oil Prices and the International Financial System. Since we were having dinner after class, I tried to stay alert. I noted that oil prices had changed the international financial system in the following ways: the Arabs had entered banking and Eurodollar markets; the foreign exchange market had become more volatile . . . then I got lost during a discussion of vertical integration and petrodollars, emerging only for the final point: currently, there's an oil glut and oil experts have been wrong.

I was wondering what on earth I had to say to this woman at dinner. We talked about Bill and Aquatect.

See you very soon!

xxM

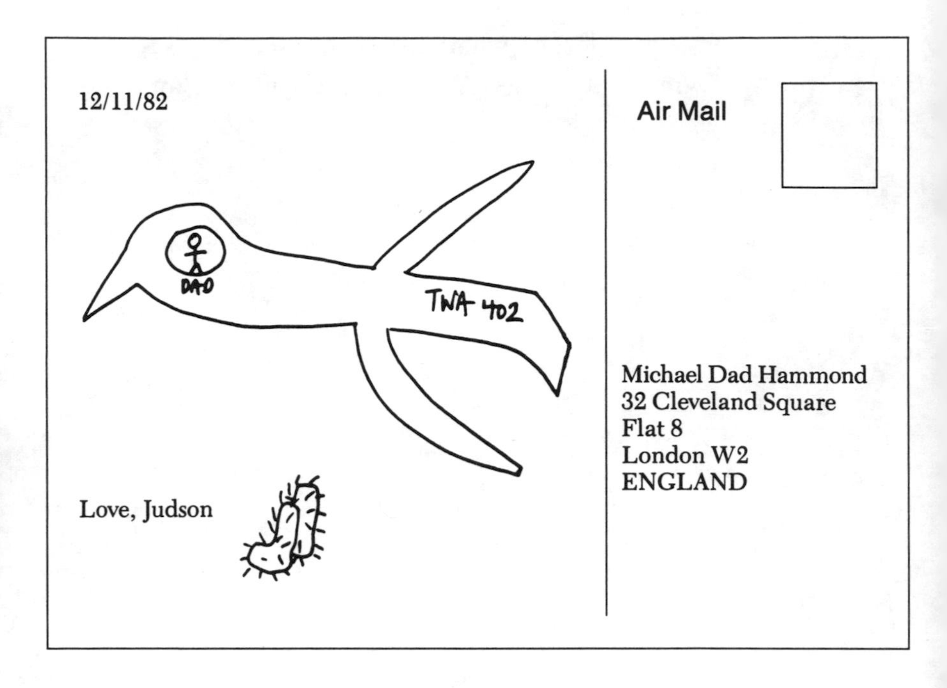
12/11/82
DAD
TWA 402
Air Mail
Michael Dad Hammond
32 Cleveland Square
Flat 8
London W2
ENGLAND
Love, Judson

Inwood Road
Pleasantville, New York

December 15, 1982

Dearest Michael,

Shall I tell you how the washing machine broke down?

First, there was a conspicuous silence, followed by a reassuring *click* into the wash cycle.

But the wash cycle never ended. After about 20 minutes, I sent Judson down to inspect. He was wearing a beard made of soapsuds when he returned. "There's soap and water all over the place!" he said.

And sure enough, our choked-up washer was exhaling bubble after bubble of unscented Tide. None of the water had drained into the sink. ALL THE WATER WAS ON THE FLOOR.

"It's my fault," Jeanne shouted, extracting a pair of fishnet pantyhose from the hose in the sink, "I forgot you're not supposed to put them in."

It took all the rags and mops in the Hammond household, combined with all the rags and mops in Elaine's and Dr. Nelson's households, to soak up the water. Jeanne recruited Terry and Josh. When they were finished, I took my little SWAT team to Carvel's, where each of them ordered a banana barge.

I have noticed, lately, that our appliances are cowardly. They act up *only* when you're away.

A very tired, Kate

SATAN SMITING JOB WITH SORE BOILS c. 1826
William Blake
Tempera on mahogany, 32 × 43.2 cm/12 7/8 × 17 in.
Tate Gallery (N.03340)

Air Mail

12/19/82

Bill—

Finally met Susan for dinner. She's quite fetching.

Why would a philosopher-king set this woman free?

Michael

Professor Bill Stern
Philosophy Hall
Columbia University
New York, New York
10027
U.S.A.

Western Union Telegram
London

12/20/82

KATE—FLIGHT CHANGE—ARRIVING JFK ON 12/24 FLIGHT 502 AT 7PM STOP LOVE MICHAEL STOP

Lent

Who's zoomin' who?
Aretha Franklin

Moorland Drive
Pleasantville, New York

January 6, 1983

Dear Kate,

Don't mean to pry, but I am concerned. I did not get harmonious feelings from the Hammond household at Christmas. Judson and Jeanne came over, cried their eyes out and, you know how it works with kids, Terry and Josh got all choked up too. A houseful of depressed children did nothing for my mood. Never mind the fact that it scared Date #32 away. My therapist said two things: (1) Something's wrong at the Hammonds; (2) Date #32 cannot handle emotion and is, therefore, the last person I need.

Please feel that you have a friend around the block. I will not try to sell you a microwave (no one wants trampolines any more).

Love, Elaine

THE DEATH OF SOCRATES
Jacques Louis David, French, 1748–1825
Oil on canvas, 1787
The Metropolitan Museum of Art

Air Mail

January 9, 1983

Qua Susan:

"Beauty is that which we cannot wish to change. It is something that one desires without wanting to devour it. We simply wish that it should be."

Simone Weil

Happy New Year, Bill

Michael Hammond
32 Cleveland Square
Flat 8
London W2
ENGLAND

Inwood Road
Pleasantville, New York

January 14, 1983

Dear Robert,

Nothing but trouble from poets—and it's *your* fault for introducing me to the man. He's in London writing his book and I'm working, taking care of the kids, watching my friends get fired at work and wondering if I'm next. And throughout all this I'm RESENTING MY OWN HUSBAND who, only recently, has begun to enjoy England.

It's not right for me to contact you only when I'm down but, if you have a free weekend, I would love to come up with the kids and show them what a cow looks like.

Love, Kate

P.S. I saw your name in the General Studies catalogue. Has Columbia asked you back?

Route 1 Hotel
South Carolina

January 15, 1983

Dear Mom,

Sorry about leaving you with the kids on such short notice. I'd much rather be with them than doing a survey of the EPA's Hazardous Waste Landfills. I'm discouraged. Thought I'd be doing *less* traveling for work but, with a leaner staff, I'm jumping like a jackrabbit these days.

After a dinner of hush puppies and slaw at Holt's Barbecue and a depressing day interviewing people sick from drinking water, I kept thinking *something has got to change.* I don't want to live like this. I got into the car, rolled up the windows so I could hear the radio and, what should be playing?—"Take This Job And Shove It," followed by "I Wish I Had a Job To Shove."

Mom, I'm so unsettled. *Don't* want to worry you but, here I am, 35 years old, with 2 kids, facing a declining film industry—and my husband (thank God it's only for a year) is in London. I think you sensed that Michael and I were having problems at Christmas. None of the combustive laughter we usually have around the house during the holiday season. Don't know what to do.

Love, Kate

Pawlet, Vermont

January 20, 1983

Mignonne!

Sois calme. Sois brave. Ne pleure pas. LE DIABLE EST MORT![*] Tu es belle, superbe, spirituelle, piquante. (Je ne te kid pas!)

What about Valentine's Day weekend? And don't forget a present—I'll be 78.

Je t'aime, Robert

[*] Yes. Columbia wants me to give a series of lectures on French Opera. Thought I'd start with Gounod's *Faust.*

Bronxville, New York

January 21, 1983

Sweetheart–

I'm happy to take care of the kids. Don't worry about *that.* Now that Pop's gone,* it does me good. But don't get me started on your situation. I sent you to college, bought you all the self-help or, at least, how-to-avert-personal-disaster books–AND WHAT DID YOU DO? Pick an unstable industry and *don't get me started* on your husband! This year, especially, he's pushed the Muse Business a little too far.

It's none of *my* business. I just want you and the kids to be happy and, as long as you're working your ass off and giving your usual 99 percent, things will be fine. I just wish you could relax.

Love, Mom

* Cursed be the day he brought home *Immortal Poems of the English language!*

COLUMBIA UNIVERSITY

Philosophy Hall
January 25, 1983

Dear Kate,

I have this image of you at work—like Murke in Heinrich Böll's story, "Murke's Collected Silences." When things get bad, you splice together the silences from a narration track you want no part of, then you play them back to yourself.

I hear that things are bad in the television world. If it were in my power to award you the silver baton at the Columbia-Dupont awards this year, I would.

Thanksgiving was wonderful. I know you didn't want me there, but it was worth putting up with your unmitigated hatred of me to chat with your mother, the Hammonds, the kids, and, what a hoot, Elaine.

I'm sure Michael told you about his dinner with Susan. She was as pleased to find a friend (she's American and is only a guest lecturer) as Michael seemed to be. Can we be friends? I dare not call you for Valentine's Day, but what do you say to having a drink, barbecue with the kids—whatever—for Groundhog's Day? That neutral enough?

Yours, Bill

P.S. Read Philip Larkin's *All What Jazz?* when you get a chance. Best line: "I never liked bop."

DR. WALTER FEINSTEIN
30 Rockefeller Plaza
New York, New York, 10020

New York

January 25, 1983

Dear Kate,

The only kind of bonding process I value is between people. That's why I refused to bond your very pretty teeth for cosmetic purposes. It's also too expensive and, given what you told me about your employment situation, not a priority.

I loved seeing you and the kids, as always. Which brings me to my original point about bonding. Gladys died before we had started a family and, in some ways, I think the grieving period would have been easier on me with that kind of support. You had mentioned that your neighbor, Elaine, might be interested in dating. If she is, I would love to take her out for Valentine's Day. Out of respect for Gladys, I have not dated a woman in 5 years. I think it's time I did.

Fondly, Walter

12 Wellington Square
Oxford, England

January 28, 1983

Dear Kate,

A few words to tell you that we arrived safely. Michael came up yesterday and took Peter Jr. off our hands. Cathy found them running in a rhombus and realized that Michael was trying to teach him baseball. Our geranium was home plate. Under Michael's expert instruction, Peter mastered the slide and knocked the innocent plant over. Foul play.

Michael has already shared his day-trip itinerary with us. In the next six months, he thinks we should be able to see the 15 sights he's researched. I reminded him that I was here to finish my book on war poets. That didn't seem to bother him. "We'll help you with it," he said, winking at Cathy. His enthusiasm is infectious—and his energy! In his next life, I see him as a Connemara pony, running sure-footed and free in some Celtic landscape.

Cathy and I (as well as Babe Peter) send our love.

xxPeter

Inwood Road
Pleasantville, New York

February 2, 1983

Dear Bill,

I don't hate you, but I am booked for Groundhog's Day, as well as Valentine's Day. If you'd like to dye Easter eggs with us, drop a note in Michael's mailbox. Or we can meet for coffee on the 12th, when I'm up at Columbia collecting his mail.

How you do persist!

Kate

Cleveland Square
London, W2

February 14, 1983

Dear Kate,

And what am I supposed to think when my wife has not written since Christmas and when I call at hours God-fearing people are in bed on Valentine's Day I get no answer?

Would you *please* be my Valentine, despite our problems (few), despite my imperfections (many), despite my selfishness (titanic)?

My quiver has *one* arrow that won't stop 'til it pins you.

M.

P.S. I've sent you the biggest chocolate heart in all the United Kingdom!

Pawlet, Vermont

February 14, 1983

Dear Michael,

Night of blue marble, softened only by a few clouds pulled like cotton across the moon. When we walk, the snow sounds like styrofoam—"Is this how I was named?" Scrunch asked.

Judson and Jeanne saw a broad-nosed cow, felt its sandpaper tongue and, curse your Robert, witnessed a heifer giving birth—a placenta so big we all got sick.

I'm sending your mail: forms for next year, and a card from Susan that arrived just after New Year's. Don't treat me like a fool. I'm not suspicious, but I've much to be suspicious about.

Last Friday was my last day at work. An uneventful end to a ten-year commitment. Cleaned out my files, drawers, turned in my credit cards, company I.D., took my stapler and tape dispenser home.

Robert, Judson and Jeanne send their love. Happy Valentine's Day.

Kate

Pawlet, Vermont

February 14, 1983

You no good bum—no better than Ulysses!

And you're gonna lose her if you keep this up—she's not the Penelope type!

Don't know what you're up to, but I *hope* Kate's doubts are unfounded. There's *none* better than Kate. And I've seen *trillions*.

Finish those damn poems and come back on your knees if you have to!

Robert

Samson with his strong body
had a weak head, or he would not
have laid it on a harlot's lap.
Ben Franklin

Moorland Drive
Pleasantville, New York

February 20, 1983

Dear Kate,

I had given up on *New York* magazine and was about to try Video Dating when Walter Feinstein, D.D.S., called. *Very* thoughtful of you to think of me and a *very nice man* Walter turned out to be. He took me to The Terrace for dinner, which you must know from your Columbia connection. *Very romantic* (very expensive!). Next weekend he wants to take the kids SKIING! Is this guy for real!?

Love, Elaine

P.S. He's *not bad* for a dentist. I normally don't date mustaches, but it makes his face stronger—kind of like a Schnauser.

12 Wellington Square
Oxford, England

February 28, 1983

Dear Kate,

Peter and I have been keeping an eye on Michael. We go to all the literary gatherings together, stay for the readings, and leave before the questions. We've met a number of poets here. They are easily distinguished by their inability to type or drive cars. They are often found with a pint of beer in hand or, if someone else is paying, a whiskey.

Last night Michael read at The Poetry Society. The women here, *starved* for red-blooded males, were not used to seeing a big, dark, healthy poet. At least five of them hovered around him after the reading. Michael was very well-behaved. In fact, he out-Brits the English sometimes with his formality. When he needs to, he says things like "Sorry . . ." *just* the way they say it. They use "Sorry" for everything and anything, so in the end it means nothing.

I wish you were here. Peter's working too hard; he's *driven*. Michael's the only one who can get him to slow down. He's very good with Peter Jr., too—they've built a pitcher's mound in the backyard.

I probably shouldn't know what happened, but I did want to say that Peter and I are very angry at your stupid Network News. Michael told us. He's worried about you and gets very frustrated when he cannot be with you as things happen.

Love,
Cathy, Peter, and peter

Hotel Berne
Paris 8e

> *But every man is tempted, when*
> *he is drawn away of his own lust,*
> *and enticed.*
>
> *Then when* lust *hath* conceived,
> *it bringeth forth* sin: *and* sin *when it*
> *is* finished, *bringeth forth* DEATH! ! !
>
> *James 1: 14–15* (*emphasis* mine)

March 1, 1983

Dearest K–

So *that's* it—JALOUSIE, as the French call it. Is that what accounts for your deafening silences? Had to leave England before I could even discuss the matter: on Easter Sunday, 1955, the Brits hanged Ruth Ellis for her crime of passion. Here she would have been made a national heroine.

Now listen—STOP THIS! I'm in this ratty hotel *alone*—satin sheets (yuk!) notwithstanding. Any tryst would have been doomed: each night at 4 AM the mail trucks from the Postes, Télégraphe, Téléphone (P.T.T.) make as much noise as the garbage trucks in Cleveland Square. The International Truckers Association is out to destroy my hearing.

More disturbing is your loss of work. I've tried to call and break through that fake self-sufficiency of yours. I know you're a wreck outside and a puddle of saltwater inside and I'm worried about you. Come to Paris, if your severance check was as generous as it should be. I'm staying for a month.

All the postcards from the Musée Rodin are too provocative to send without envelopes. I enclose *L'Eternelle Idole* (1889)—the one of me making the moves on you while you're picking your toe.

Love to you, Judson, and Jeanne,
Michael

Hotel Berne
Paris 8e

March 17, 1983

Dear Sham Rock,

I guess you're not coming. The fountains at the Place de la Concorde have stopped dancing and the Obelisk has lost its point. The only green I saw was in the Metro—an ugly old woman wearing much-too-much eyeshadow, as if, 20 years ago, the only person who had ever noticed her had once said, "Green is your color."

Ah, but *Spring is i-cumen in—Lhude sing, cuccu!* The parrot in the window across the way is swaying like Stevie Wonder!

I miss you, but can feel your chill 3000 miles away. If we are to be formal, I enclose an Ambassador I found in the Parc Monceau—a crocus wearing a white suit with lavender pinstripes. *Très correct.*

Love, M.

Inwood Road
Pleasantville, New York

March 30, 1983

Dear M—

Last Saturday, Elaine invited me to brunch:

JOIN ME
AND
15
FASCINATING
SUCCESSFUL
WOMEN
(LIKE YOU!)
FOR BRUNCH
(AND A LITTLE NETWORKING!)

Maybe she's anticipating the collapse of our marriage because it was really a rap session about men. Whatever her reasons, she always confronts me with situations that are not mine, but that could have been. What I mean is that there were 13 attractive, intelligent, successful, kind women who *can* live alone, but who would *prefer* not to. And that seems reasonable. But New York City, where most of them live, presents them with unreasonable circumstances. The supply of women exceeds the demand. It's also impossible for a single woman to afford an apartment if she wants to live alone and, because the average age of the group was 37, the roommate years are over. Yet for professional and social reasons, it seems essential that these women live in New York. I think

I am faithfully reporting the themes. Then there are the specific cases:

Phyllis, the Real Estate Agent—"The way I see it is that we are all 2-million-dollar townhouses—very difficult to sell."

Judy, the Chief Executive Officer of a Fortune 500 Company—"I only date Chief Executive Officers."

Deb, the President of her own Advertising Agency—"I work hard, but that's the deal. Most men won't put up with it. But I asked myself 'Do you want to be 60 and eat dog food?' "

Sue, a human resources manager at AT&T—"My Tarot Cards looked good this week, so I should be meeting someone soon."

Cathy, the Banker—"I've given up on men. I'm running in this year's marathon."

Bette, an editor at Random House—"I want kids."

Alice, a lawyer at Coudert—"I've dated every eligible man in the firm."

Claire, a writer—"After breaking up with John, I had to move out to Queens. And the rent is still too much for me to afford."

ETC.

The only other *married* woman there wanted to talk about Volvos, "the safest car if you have kids" (she had none). I told her that we had managed to raise two kids with a 1964 heap that bore some resemblance to the original Cadillac. As if kids hadn't survived before Volvos! Just as she was starting in on cleaning ladies and daycare, Elaine announced that things were going well between her and Walter Feinstein, D.D.S.

That Sunday, Bill (he's harmless) came over to color Easter eggs. He favors green, color of hope, and his real talent emerged when it came to constructing the cardboard characters included in the kit. Very complicated instructions: "Insert Tab A into Tab C and *make sure Tab B is perforated before the Rabbit's ears are added!*"

Jeanne has developed an ostrich-egg-sized crush on Bill. Do you think my elbows are unattractive, she asked. "No, but they do look like peach pits," he replied. Poor Scrunch, I'll have to introduce her to hand and elbow creams early on, given the way she bangs her body around.

As far as my severance check is concerned, I'd like to take the kids to North Carolina for their spring break. I think it will do them good—and your brother says it's fine for us to use the house. Also, Jeanne has been saying for a long time that she'd like to take piano lessons. Part of this has to do with Judson's having ideas above his station. He says he needs An Acumpianist. Elaine says Jeanne can practice on her piano, which will save me from hearing Bach's *Minuet in G* thirteen thousand times a day. After all this, I'll put most of the money into a high-interest savings account and look for work. (This may come as a shock to you, but your wife is not and never will be a multimillionaire.)

As for you and Susan, I honestly don't want to know what is happening unless it affects us—in which case, I have a right to know. I love you, I want to believe you. But when Bill tells me (as he is smushing a marshmallow bunny into his mouth) that he has just gotten a postcard from Susan "who was recently in Paris," I don't know what to think. And of course, I still wonder why you postponed your flight home for Christmas.

Kate

P.S. The Ambassador was Dead-On-Arrival.

THE WOMEN OF AMPHISSA, 1887
Sir Lawrence Alma-Tadema, British 1836–1912
Oil on canvas, 48 × 72 inches
Sterling and Francine Clark Art Institute
Williamstown, Massachusetts

4/1/83

Dear Kate—

May I take you out to dinner on your birthday?

Bill

Kate Hammond
12 Inwood Road
Pleasantville, New York
10570

Liverpool, England

April 2, 1983

Dearest Kate,

Wish you were here to advise me. Peter and I know nothing about horses. Just go by their names. Rupertino, Austerlitz and Tsarevich got my money. Those who follow The Grand National told me As Time Goes By was the one to watch, but the would-be prize winner didn't clear the first fence (*terrible* fall). "The Chair," a jump measuring 5 feet 2 inches, with an open ditch yawning 6 feet, claimed my Rupertino.

Lousy weather for horses and people. You would not believe how devoted English spectators are. Many came hours before the race to secure parking places next to the course. During that time, they were drenched by rain, pelted by hail and, for 3 glorious minutes, sunkissed between thunderclouds. All stood firm, anchored by the vast quantities of bitter, bangers and Gloucester cheese they had consumed from picnic spreads in the trunks of their cars.

Peter and I bought fish and chips; then, like everybody else, we surveyed the four-and-a-half-mile course. The ground was sucking wet and we had little experience walking in "Wellies." The boots knew this and humiliated us by sounding off mucky farts with every step.

When the horses ran, we were a few yards away,

watching from the ground—How magnificent (and frightening) the cavalries must have been!

(Tsarevich won.)

Love, M.

THE BABYLONIAN MARRIAGE MARKET
University of London, Canvas 68 × 120 in
Edwin Long, R.A. (1829–1891).
In 1875 this painting created a sensation at the Royal Academy. The artist's inspiration came from a translation of Herodotus in which the Babylonian custom of obtaining wives by auction is described.

Air Mail

4/6/83

Dear Elaine,

Kate told me about the dentist.
Shall I rent a tuxedo?

Regards, Michael Hammond

Elaine Letucci
185 Moorland Drive
Pleasantville, New York
10570
U.S.A.

Inwood Road
Pleasantville, New York

April 8, 1983

Dear Michael,

While you were at the races with Peter, I was doing our taxes. Sifting through a year's worth of receipts put me in a very bad mood. So bad that I snapped at Sidney for the first time. It went like this:

"Why aren't you claiming any deductions that are automatically allowed?"

"Like what?" I asked.

"Sidewalk Santas, the church collection plate—that sort of thing."

"Because I don't give to Sidewalk Santas and I don't go to church."

"Doesn't matter. It's automatic for Catholics. The IRS won't check."

"Sidney?"

"What?"

"NO collection plates and NO Santas—just remember to deduct yourself this year!"

Sidney called back to ask if he had said anything wrong. I apologized and told him that you were away for the year and that I was stuck with the taxes. "You're a schnook," he said. And he's right.

It's *your* turn next year. I wonder if your Tsarevich winnings is considered taxable income.

Love, Kate

Pawlet, Vermont

April 14, 1983

Dear Kate—

Don't know what you've been writing Michael, but the man's running scared. You might want to back off a bit, unless, of course, you have proof—photographs, fingerprints—in which case *I'll kill him.*

The only woman I know who ever sent a detective to investigate her husband's infidelity found out that her husband was having an affair with another *man* (a Priest!). Oh Dear.

Love, Robert

COLUMBIA UNIVERSITY

Philosophy Hall

April 16, 1983

Dearest Kate—

I'm somewhat obtuse when it comes to women, but I do know one thing: when a married woman cries after making love, chances are she's still in love with her husband. Judging by the way you cried, I would say very much in love.

I'm sorry I left early, but I was feeling very much alone next to someone I've always loved, who has always loved someone else.

Please don't worry about the children. I didn't put my shoes on until I was well past the driveway.

And don't be ashamed: "It's only in mediocre books that people are divided into two camps and have nothing to do with each other" (Pasternak).

Michael's a lucky man. Happy Birthday.

Love, Bill

Moorland Drive
Pleasantville, New York

April 16, 1983

Dear Kate,

Don't you hate women who remember your 36th birthday, especially when they're a few months younger?

Have a Happy one. Gotta rush—Walter is leaving for work and wants to drop off the attached present. Hope you like it.* If nothing else, it will convince you that defrosting (not cooking) is the way to go.

Love, Elaine

* Consider it your finder's fee for getting me a husband!

Cleveland Square
London, W2

HAPPY BIRTHDAY*
(I'll call tonight)

April 16, 1983

Dear Kate—

Look, I'm sorry about Phyllis, Judy, Deb, Sue, Cathy, Bette, Alice and Claire—but aside from providing you with material for a documentary, which is what the first part of your letter sounded like, I'm not sure what they offer you. And frankly, I'm still reeling from lines like "Maybe Elaine's anticipating the collapse of our marriage." What possessed you, Bruiser, to punch that against the page?

You're hurting me. Susan (*she's* harmless) is a friend. Yes, she was in Paris for one of the weeks I was there and, yes, I did not mention it, precisely because I know how your imagination reacts to facts—like a frying pan to drops of water. As for TWA Flight 402, I missed it because I had to meet with my editor at Queen's Press. I'm sure I told you that at Christmas, but when your mind goes into its self-righteous mode, it is remarkably infertile.

I'm not wild about the way Bill resurrected on Easter, but I guess it's unfair of me to comment if I'm expecting you to accept my friendship (one I would *gladly* forfeit) with Susan. This said, I just wanted to add that I'm not wild about the way Bill resurrected on Easter. And what I really cannot fathom is why he's after my wife instead of Susan. By that I mean, Susan's available.

I'm happy for Elaine and Walter, but I'm even more enthusiastic about our little trumpet and piano team.

Hope your trip to Nags Head does the trick. Say hello to Mack, who sells fishing line at the pier, and to Hazel, the cleaning lady at the Beachcomber Motel. I've known them since I was six—feels odd that it's your first time down and I'm not with you.

xxMichael

* As one of your presents, I *promise* to do next year's taxes.

Cleveland Square
London, W2

April 16, 1983—1 AM

Dearest Kate—

I've just hung up and I have a horrible feeling that something is wrong. You didn't sound yourself. Perhaps it's Miss Holliday's phone that distances you even more, but I don't think so.

By the time you get this, you'll have returned from the Outer Banks. Maybe that's all you need—a good rest. I hope you break up the distance, as I suggested. Even truckers think twice about driving eleven hours in one stretch.

All my love, Michael

Nags Head, North Carolina

April 20, 1983

Dear Daddy,

I sneaked out the back door, careful not to let the screen door slam because Mom's been crying a lot and needs to sleep. Then I crossed the blacktop that feels like shammy on my feet. There was grass on the beach that stings my ankles and I had to watch out for planks with rusty nails.

I started walking to Macks pier and because there was a storm last night lots of razor shells and jelly fish were in the way. When I got there I wish I had waited for Judson so he could see the sharks and marlins on the walls.

I asked Sam and Mack if they would let me on the pier. They said they didn't let yankees on. But Sam stamped a PAID on my wrist even though I didn't pay.

I don't know how Judson got in but he was already there. He tripped over a pail and let all this mans crabs go free and the crabs started fighting. He laughed and we stayed with him until he caught a blue. His name is Skip.

Skip let Judson try. He said to watch the maroon patch in the water. When it came near Judson's line, the line started buzzing and spinning. Skip took over but let Judson take the blue off the hook. Judson said it was slippery and the fish got away through a crack in the pier. The lady next to Skip started laughing and scared me because her gums looked like black licorish. Judson looked into her pail and poked a fish. Don't fool with it! she yelled. She told him it was dead plain and simple.

In the afternoon we went to see your friend Hazel. Judson says he wants to tell you about that. But first we went back to the cottage for lunch to see Mom. I really wish you would finish your book.

Love, Jeanne

Nags Head, North Carolina

April 20, 1983

Dear Dad,

The Beachcomber has a pool that Hazel lets us use. Scrunch said Lets pretend we're otters so the surface won't ripple but I wanted to play Marco Polo. Then Hazel gave us quarters to buy orange Crush in the machine. She took us into a room she was cleaning. Before she made the beds Hazel showed us how to put quarters in the Magic Fingers machine and make the bed shake. She said it was the dumbest thing she had ever seen and the biggest waste of money but the box had to be emptied every week it got so full.

I got a sunburn the first day and Mom says I have to wear a T-shirt.

Love, Judson

P.S. I made a friend Skip at the pier. He showed me how to catch blues but mine got away. I wish you were here.

Nags Head, North Carolina

April 22, 1983

Dearest M—

We ended up taking a two-day roundabout route to get here, veering off the highway when we got bored with asphalt and signs for Stuckey's pecan rolls. Judson and Jeanne kept a list of their favorite spots—The Shangrila mobile park; Honeycutt's Taxidermy; Madam Eden, palmist; Bethel Baptist Church; the U.S. Tobacco Company, with huge packs of Carlton and Tareyton outside the plant; Lee's headquarters at Fredricksburg and Neptune's Gallery restaurant with a barge-size figure of Neptune on top. I liked the kudzu vines that smell like grape soda and dress even telephone poles in green sequins.

The water's not warm enough for swimming. Only Hazel has the courage to go in. Each morning, she gets up at 6 AM, drinks a glass of water containing three drops of vinegar, puts her hair in curlers, and lets the waves smack her around for 15 minutes. If scientists could put Hazel's and Robert's genes together, they'd crack the code for immortality.

Why isn't Mike here, Hazel asks from time to time, and I explain that you're writing a book in London. Waste of time, she mutters.

Judson and Scrunch are either at the pool, on the pier, or sitting in the surf. They sit like miniature dams until the water carves irrigation channels around their legs and forces sand into their bathing suits, at which point they dive into the water and rinse it all out. It's the bubble-holes that transfix them. Just when they think the sea has erased them, the sand spits up more and Judson, especially, digs for the source—usually a flailing sand crab.

I've been taking long walks and sleeping a great deal. Probably too much. I think about how this year is botching up things for us. I remind myself that it is only a year.

Thanks for calling on my birthday. I'm sorry I was so tired, dull and weepy.

All my love, Kate

Cleveland Square
London, W2

April 23, 1983

Dearest Kate,

Pissy weather. Wind gusts that snap umbrella wings and paste leaves to the sidewalk. Learned what an "Incident" means in the tube. Every day, they announce Incidents at Oxford Circus, Incidents at Piccadilly. I've assumed they refer to subway fires. Not so. Not always. Today at Tottenham Court Road, London Transport announced, "Due to someone under the train, there will be a seven minute delay on the Central Line."

Can't tell you how depressed I've been all day. With each "Incident," I wonder if someone might be derailing a life in this mythically shitty climate.

Day after day goes by with *no hope* for even the most persistent sunbeam!* Peter and Cathy are in France.

I miss you, and find myself rereading your letters, slowly, as letters should be read.

Michael

* Hope you are having better weather in Nags Head!

Moorland Drive
Pleasantville, New York
April 25, 1983

Elaine Letucci
is pleased to announce

her marriage

to Walter Feinstein, D.D.S.

The ceremony
will be held at 2 PM on May 23
at Our Lady of Fatima Church
on Garth Road
in Pleasantville

Reception to follow
at the Pleasantville Country Club

P.S. Walter noticed a man in socks near the foot of your driveway when he dropped off your birthday present. I hope you're using the alarm system.

P.P.S. I've invited Bill so you'll have someone to dance with!

Isola del Giglio

(Sunny!)
Italia

May 2, 1983

Bella Katerina—

Thanks to the classified ads in the *International Herald Tribune*, I find myself sharing a vacation house with an Italian couple and their eight-year-old son, Vincenzo. Beatrice and Paolo have something that I hesitate to call a relationship—it's something that sticks and carries them through the day, but it has nothing to do with love. They eat together and spend most of their day watching Vincenzo, who chatters, sings to himself, and screams ZANZARONE! every time a mosquito bites his bare body.

I'm writing from our terrace, which overlooks the aqua marine—whoever coined the color must have been looking at the Mediterranean. Surrounding me are white oleanders, olive trees, and fuscia Bougainvillaea, but it's the geraniums in front of me that are sturdiest against the wind. A black beetle just parked on my toe and a lizard passed by in a very big hurry. Only the people here don't look purposeful.

I love this land of caffé latte, caffé lungo, cappuccino, caffé freddo and caffé Hag. There's nothing we've botched, as you put it, and my book gets fatter by the days. Thank Judson and Jeanne for their beautiful letters.

xxM

Summer

I had a sister much older than myself,
from whose modesty and goodness, which were great,
I learned nothing.

Saint Teresa

CHILDREN'S TELEVISION NETWORK

New York, New York

May 10, 1983

Dear Kate.

I was sorry to hear about the bloodbath at your network, but I think I can help you. It might mean putting aside the issues you care about—Central America, nuclear proliferation, toxic chemicals, etc. But from what I hear, nobody has the forum to do that kind of work anymore.

Which brings me to the subject of sea cows. For our science series, we need someone (you) to produce a one-hour show on manatees. I enclose a picture of the mammal, who is nearly extinct. If you accept the job, you will need to spend about two weeks shooting in Florida, where most of them live.

I think you could do a good job on this and have a blast doing it!

Regards,
Adele Harris

Inwood Road
Pleasantville, New York

May 11, 1983

Dear Elaine,

Congratulations!!!!!!!!!!!!!!!!!!!!!!!!!!!!

What great news and of course I'll come!

Please don't feel that you have to invite Bill for me. It's time I taught Judson to fox-trot.

Love, Kate

P.S. Thanks again for the microwave, a far too generous present. Haven't succeeded in trying any recipes. Judson and Jeanne are constantly using it to pop corn.

THE MANATEE, or sea cow, was once abundant in Florida coastal waters, but now only 1000 remain. These gentlest of all animals, once hunted to near extinction, now face a new enemy—the cutting blades of powercraft that ply Florida waterways. A vegetarian, the manatee helps control the growth of water plants that clog waterways.

5/20/83

Spent 4 hours waiting for this lardball to surface and, when he did, he didn't bother to lift his head—just floated along at a clipping speed of 10 feet per hour. That's fine for a survey trip, but what about when I'm paying a cameraman $550/day? At that point I'll finish like Ahab harpooned to the massive cow. As for the manatee, extinction would be too kind.

Tonight I fly back for Elaine's wedding. Morale is better. I miss you and love you very much.

Kate

Pub by Gabor Card Co., 14880 Cleveland Ave., Ft. Myers, FL 33908

Air Mail

Mr. Michael Hammond
32 Cleveland Square
Flat 8
London W2
ENGLAND

Cleveland Square
London, W2

May 27, 1983

Dearest K–

God help the manatee! When you get through with him, the poor mammal might have been better off extinct. Remember that the show is for children and is not another nursing home scam. So none of this: THE MANATEE: ANATOMY OF AN EXTINCTION. Or worse still: WHO WILL SPEAK FOR THE MANATEE?

But OH I'm glad you're back in the saddle. All the rest will fall into place, my manic darling. Can't wait to hear about Elaine's ceremony. First question: How the hell did a divorcée get Father Murphy to marry her to a Jew in a Catholic church? Susan tells me that Bill was invited, but had plans to visit her in London. Nice of Elaine to include him, but I prefer to have him on this side of the Atlantic, where I can keep my eyes on him and, next week, interrogate him about my wife.

Maybe he'll come to his senses and marry Susan.

Love, M

Inwood Road
Pleasantville, New York

June 2, 1983

Dearest M—

The bride wore white. The groom wore a tux. Nobody knows how Elaine pulled it off in the church. Rumors about greasing the collection plate circulated, but nobody who knew Elaine well (almost everybody) took them seriously.

They even had a mass. During communion, Judson asked rather loudly How come Father Murphy gets such a big wafer? Then he told Jeanne, who had just received the body of Christ, that she would go straight to hell because she hadn't gone to confession. She whispered that she felt clean inside.

Hope your dinner with Bill and Susan went well. And I agree—they should marry.

Love, K.

P.S. Ran into Dr. Nelson and his wife, Joan, at the wedding. They're stopping in London before going to Cornwall and would like to take you to tea at Brown's.

Cleveland Square
London, W2

June 15, 1983

Dearest Kate—

Have you ever seen the tulips behind Hampton Court!? King's Blood, Balalaika, Eros, President Kennedy, and Gordon Cooper (who he?). After yesterday's visit, my dreams were *pointillist!*

Thanks for your brief summary of Elaine's wedding. I don't know if Bill and Susan will make it to the altar. We had dinner at Monsoon, an Indian restaurant on Westbourne Grove, and they seemed happy enough to see each other, but Bill was extremely standoffish.

I finally got the story of how they met. Bill had been teaching a seminar on business ethics and Susan, a professor at the Yale School of Management, was the guest speaker. At dinner last night, they started discussing "collective responsibility." Bill thinks that institutions are incapable of acting as moral agents; Susan believes they can. Their only other point of disagreement was how much curry they wanted in the *chicken tikka masala* they were sharing. Nothing insurmountable.

Bill ribbed me on the subject of modern poetry, calling modern poets miniaturists. Don't get me wrong, he reassured me, you're no less competent artistically (what a relief), it's just that you're less bold metaphysically, he said. He asked what had happened to The Great Themes—had the older generation of poets exhausted them? But how can you exhaust love and death, he asked.

We then went to Pinter's play, *Betrayal,* and afterwards, over several brandys (Susan left after the first), Bill confessed that he had taken you out for your birthday. I vaguely remember saying that since I was a selfish sonofabitch who, at my wife's expense, was having a quiet, productive year in London, I thought he had done the right thing and I thanked him for it. You see, darling, how your jealous husband has reformed. Besides, I'm beginning to like the guy.

Got a letter from Hunter, Stein today, giving me a December deadline for my manuscript. I need your advice on a title. My editor's keen on *Green Park,* to place most of the poems in London. Having just finished my best bird poem, I'm tempted to call it *A Murder of Crows And Other Stories.* You'll probably want me to name it after one of the love poems, in which case I would worry about it ending up in a supermarket rack, above the Bazooka and next to the *Inquirer.*

Hope the manatee surfaced for you. Look forward to seeing Dr. and Mrs. Nelson.

All my love, Michael

Cleveland Square
London, W2

June 18, 1983

Dear Kate,

Poor Miss Holliday's losing her mind. Last night she came by to wish me pleasant dreams. That's not unusual, but this time she was wearing lipstick. "I put it on at 11 PM in case I have an unexpected rendezvous with my maker," she said. She also explained the strange noise I've been hearing for the past month—"Before going to sleep, I roll two ping-pong balls under the bed to make sure no men are hiding there."

Very sudden, this decline into her second childishness.

Love, M.

Inwood Road
Pleasantville, New York

June 19, 1983

Dear Daddy,

SCHOOL's OVER!!!!!!!!!!!!!

I still have to practice the piano with Miss Hans. But I love her and she just taught me the F clef. I can play with both hands not very well.

Judson and I will probably go to day camp. And you'll be HOME!!!!!!!!!

Love, love, love X X X X,
Jeanne

Bronxville, New York

June 20, 1983

Dear Kate,

You don't let me talk over the phone because you never want to hear what hurts. My first concern is you, as well as Judson and Jeanne.

All I wanted to know the other day was whether Shakespeare had committed himself to coming home. Paris, Italy—it's all very nice and I'm sure he has a few verses to show for it, but if he was really any good would he have to displace himself so much? "When I feel the need to travel, I just close my eyes." That's Emily Dickinson. But of course Michael doesn't have the good sense to like her work. He gave me that beautiful two-volume biography about her last Christmas and, don't know if he showed you, inscribed:

To—Mom
With—love!
From—Michael
For—Christmas!

You could have married any man you wanted and instead you chose a very difficult life. How are you managing financially and how the hell can he *afford* a year's sabbatical? If your father were alive, he'd bury Michael under a bookcase.

All my love, Mom

12 Wellington Square
Oxford, England

June 21, 1983

Dear Kate,

Michael said we couldn't leave England without seeing Stonehenge. So we rented a car and drove straight into a detour. How were we to know it was summer solstice? We were routed 30 miles out of our way and, when the pile of rubble was finally in sight, an officer stopped us.

"What's the problem, officer?" Michael asked in the most deferential tone I have *ever* heard come from his mouth.

"Druids," the officer replied. "We've cordoned off the site."

From where we were, we could see the coppers, in their polite, sadistic manner, dragging Druids away as if they were demonstrators from Greenham Common.

I won't be sorry to leave England. Peter's accomplished most of what he set out to do. Now I want him to relax.

Whenever I think of how insanely in love with Peter I am, I think of you and Michael. Not too many women have what we have.

Love,
Cathy (and Peter and peter)

Pawlet, Vermont

June 25, 1983

Dear Kate,

Did you find work? Was reading the classifieds and saw a want ad for a dairy farmer. They're willing to train and can accommodate the family in a one-bedroom with a parlor. Don't worry about clients—I can round up the heifers that, despite technological advances in the field of mechanical insemination, *still* come to visit my bull, André.

Faust was a smash. Next lecture on Rimbaud and Verlaine for a New School series on Human Sexuality in Literature. What *won't* they dig up!?

Hope you and Michael are back on track,

Love, Robert

Inwood Road
Pleasantville, New York

June 28, 1983

Dear Michael,

Last night I was cutting the opening sequence to Manatee. Adele insisted we use state-of-the-art video graphics; so Joe, the editor, and I played with the "paintbox" and special effects until we came up with something that pleased everybody. After one particularly inspired cut, I told Joe he was doing fine work. He turned around, smiled, and said, "You see, I'm a poet too."

And of course that remark started me thinking about you. No matter how busy I am—and I'm often busier than you—I always find time to think about you. I don't think I'm alone among women. In fact, I count myself among the women who resent men for their powers of concentration. This does not mean that we are not as good at what we do, or that we cannot concentrate, but it does make us envy men for their ability to focus *only* on their work.

Maybe we were brought up in a way that forbade that kind of selfishness. All I know is that this envy, coupled with rage, accounts for many of the moods and some of the behavior I have experienced since you've been away. I have my own work and the children to keep me busy but, somehow, I do not sufficiently value what I do. I feel that I am constantly accommodating you. What angers me is that I have to take on much more than you—work, children, household responsibilities—in order to lighten your burden so you can write and teach.

This does not mean that I love you less, but it does mean that we have to sort things out. I'll begin with myself.

I know this comes suddenly for you. For me, it's been welling up for a while. I don't know how this will affect us. To some extent it has already changed me. That's what happens when you marry students; they turn on you and grow into women.

All my love,
Kate

Cleveland Square
London, W2

July 4, 1983

Dear Kate,

Your letter arrived today. If Dr. Nelson had not met me for tea yesterday, I would not have been able to decipher it. He had just finished his first scone when he mentioned that Elaine was concerned about security in the neighborhood. Why, I asked. Because Walter spotted a man in socks near the front of your driveway. Really? . . . When? On April 16th, he remembered, because it was his wife's birthday. That's funny, I said, because Kate was born on the 16th as well. What time did you see him, I asked. Early morning, he replied. And, of course, with this last bit of information, I lost my taste for tea and scones.

In fact, I've lost my appetite for just about everything. You have a distorted sense of my self-sufficiency. Maybe I function best in the very context I can no longer take for granted.

I wish you had discussed what was bothering you before you retaliated in a way I doubt was of any satisfaction to you. Susan had nothing to do with the problems you were struggling with.

You should have trusted me.
M.

CHILDREN'S TELEVISION NETWORK

New York, New York

July 14, 1983

Dear Kate,

We were so pleased with Manatee that we want to offer you more work. This time on the excavations at Herculaneum. The Smithsonian has film rights, but they are allowing us to coproduce a film for our science series. So what we need is a coordinating producer. This suits you fine because you can do most of the work from New York and don't have to leave the kids.

I've been to Herculaneum, which is outside of Naples, and it really is extraordinary. It's a seaside resort that was covered in the AD 79 eruption that buried Pompeii. Italian workmen have unearthed slaves, soldiers, and a couple locked by lava in their last embrace.

Let me know if you are interested,
Adele Harris

Inwood Road
Pleasantville, New York

July 16, 1983

Dearest M—

I've been calling you for days. Don't know where you are and want to assure you that what happened was a symptom and not the cause of what I have been going through.

I'm confused. In the same way you make time for yourself through your work, I need to sort things out without feeling that I'm being either selfish, wrong, or insane.

Judson and Jeanne are well and have no sense of my miasmic moods. I enclose their letters. They asked if you were coming home.

All my love, K.

Inwood Road
Pleasantville, New York

July 16, 1983

Dad–

In day camp we made kites but there was no wind. Then we went swimming at saxon woods pool and Stu Bush got taken out of the water because he peed in it. Scrunch told me not to do it today because they are using the kemical that turns the water red. But I didn't tell Stu.

Love, Judson

Inwood Road
Pleasantville, New York

July 16, 1983

Dear Daddy,

Stu Bush is disgusting and we might not be able to swim at Saxon Woods because of him. It's very hot, but Walter bought Mrs. Letucci a new sprinkler that she lets us use. It's a long green plastic ribbon with pin pricks that make the water come out like a water pik.

We have been waiting a long time for you to finish your book and while you have been away things are not the same. I think you should come back so things will be better again.

Love, Jeanne

Fowey, Cornwall

July 20, 1983

Dear Robert,

Twenty-five-thousand shipwrecks here. I feel right at home. Kate's made a cuckold of me and you're the only man I can turn to. Do you know the feeling at waking—of not belonging anywhere? Have you ever closed your eyes at night and imagined your wife responding to another man's touch?!

You know the fellow. The amiable Bill Stern. How can I face him at Columbia? Did Kate actually believe that Susan and I were fucking!?

Michael

Cleveland Square
London, W2

July 25, 1983

Dear Mr. Hammond,

Not in good form, lately. Don't know if you've noticed. The milk bottles have accumulated outside the front door. Would you mind terribly if I ask you to bring them up for me? Honey could use some more cat food as well. Weakness has shamed me into depending on people more than I would normally require. The doctor says I've got pneumonia.

Miss Holliday

Cleveland Square
London, W2

July 26, 1983

Dear Kate,

I'm very sad. Miss Holliday died suddenly last night of pneumonia. She left no husband, no family—only her cat, Honey, and a devoted group of former tenants, whom she listed on the Kleenex box Dr. Simon found on her bedside table. Dr. Simon asked me if I would contact the 15 or so people (Miss Holliday left telephone numbers). I told him I would. The only other official business is legal. The executor of Miss Holliday's will tells me that, though she lived frugally, Miss Holliday was a wealthy woman.

I don't know how to respond to your needs. I accept that you have them and that you need to devote time to them. The rest is uncharted territory—only you have the compass, only you will know when you have arrived. And though you have been feeling a bit lost, I cannot forgive you for what happened. At least not right now.

I'm putting together my syllabus for this year and, honestly, I dread the situation you've created through your affair with Bill. You've made a fool out of me and I will have to confront that fact every day at Columbia.

My flight to New York is scheduled for August 21st. We'll discuss this further when I get back.

Love,
Michael

Pawlet, Vermont

August 4, 1983

Dear Kate,

Why don't you and the children come up before school starts? I've had a dead mouse in the walls for a week but, by next Friday, the ten-day smell should be gone. Hope to see you then.

Love, Robert

Grays Inn
High Holborn

August 5, 1983

Dear Mr. Hammond,

It has come to our attention that Miss Amanda Holliday left a considerable amount of money to be divided equally among her former tenants. We ask that each tenant claim the sum of 2,000 pounds no later than December 31. Please report to my office on High Holborn at your earliest convenience.

James Brooke, Solicitor

Inwood Road
Pleasantville, New York

August 14, 1983

Dearest Michael,

I don't think we should try to resolve all this by phone or letter. Distance has distorted everything. I see no reason to let that continue.

Robert has invited me and the kids up for the weekend. Look forward to that and to seeing you on the 21st.

Love, Kate

COLUMBIA UNIVERSITY

Philosophy Hall

August 19, 1983

Dear Kate,

I've been pretty good about not calling and not writing, but I find it very difficult. I'm putting together a course on Love as a Philosophical Concept and, so far, only Rousseau—whom I never liked—has helped me reconcile Reason and Passion:

> Human understanding owes much to the passions. . . . It is by their activity that our reason is perfected; we seek to know only because we desire to have pleasure and it is impossible to conceive why one who had neither desires nor fears would go to the trouble of reasoning. The passions in turn derive their origin from our needs, and their progress from our knowledge.

My Eros (passion) and Sophia (knowledge) have not been advancing at the same rate since I last saw you. Among the poets, Theodore Roethke (also on the course syllabus) expresses Rousseau's point a different way:

> *I learn by going where I have to go.*
> *We think by feeling. What else is there to know?*

I feel that I need to talk to you before Michael starts teaching. I've never been so confused. At my bedside are works by philosophers I used to dismiss as intellectually soft. Now I find them human and helpful.

Michael did his best to renew my interest in Susan (we had a fleeting enthusiasm for each other before she left for England), but I'm afraid my heart's just not in it.

A few weeks ago I bumped into Robert, who told me he was reading Rimbaud and Verlaine ("a couple of French fag poets") in preparation for a lecture at the New School. He also said that he had heard from Michael, who was touring Cornwall. Susan must have told Michael about her trip in July; she was dazzled by the area.

Please let me talk with you,

Bill

Part Two

NEW YORK

First Semester

If you find him sad,
Say I am dancing; if in mirth, report
That I am sudden sick.

Shakespeare
Antony and Cleopatra, iii. 3

300 Riverside Drive
New York City

September 17, 1983

Dear Kate,

This move is painful. I hope it's the right thing for now. I understand why you and the children did not want to be there—only movers should be present. The ones I used made a tourniquet of sentiment. They twistie-sealed my clothes and bedding into black plastic leaf bags. Part of me is suffocating along with my possessions.

Love, Michael

(I left one trunk filled with books, which I'll get another time.)

Moorland Drive
Pleasantville, New York

September 20, 1983

Dear Kate,

I'm sending this note back with Judson. If he hadn't come over to borrow Josh's basketball, I never would have known that Michael moved out. And that makes me *MAD*. The poor kid could barely dribble straight he was so depressed.

I know you're smarter than I am, but I happen to have a lot of expertise in these matters. This Sunday I'll have Walter take Josh, Terry, Judson, and Jeanne to *The Sound of Music*, whether they want to go or not. While 200 kids are throwing popcorn at Walter's head, we can talk.

If you refuse this offer I will bomb your house.

Love, Elaine

300 Riverside Drive
New York City

October 2, 1983

Dear Kate,

This morning I heard the metal sputter of briefcases being opened. I looked at the clock, which read 7:30 AM, and realized that I had been dreaming about my 7:32 train from Pleasantville. Can't say that I miss the commute. But I do miss you and the children desperately.

I got up and reviewed Coleridge (my turn to teach English 101 this year). Went to class and, halfway through our discussion of "The Rime of the Ancient Mariner," a spam-faced 17 year old piped up, "Mr. Hammond, Mr. Hammond—I *know* why it was bad luck for the Mariner to shoot the Albatross!" All eyes upon him. "It all ties into the wedding feast— You see, the Albatross mates for life!"

Somehow I made it to the cafeteria for breakfast without calling attention to the bird around my neck. Did my best to avoid Bill, who was talking constitutional law with our new Dean, but he motioned me over for a discussion of The Motherfucker Trilogy—a series of First Amendment cases that, for the most part, upheld a demonstrator's right to say fuck and pig to police officers in the sixties. I was really not in the mood for this conversation. Kept on thinking: Does Bill know I know? I excused myself by telling Bill I was waiting for Peter Clare, but even this proved unsuccessful. Peter's ill, I was told, which struck me as unlikely since I had had lunch with him the day before.

This afternoon I learned that Peter was, indeed, ill. Nobody knows what he's got and Cathy took him to Mt. Sinai for tests. The School of General Studies has asked me to teach his poetry workshop until he gets back on his feet. I've just come from the first class, which attracted the usual 9 to 3 ratio of hypersensitive women to bearded men in earth shoes. I know they come straight from work, which suggests some commitment to poetry—but, just to be sure, I'll assign them a sestina next week to weed out the less serious writers.

See you this weekend.
Love, Michael

P.S. I guess Elaine told Walter she disapproved of my move . . . Last week he drilled through my bicuspid with the delicacy of a construction worker.

Inwood Road
Pleasantville, New York

October 10, 1983

Dear Michael,

I had mixed feelings after seeing you this weekend. On the one hand, I love you, I want to be with you, I want Judson and Jeanne to spend time with you. On the other hand, I resent you for moving out. So when I have my cloudbursts, as you call them, it's because I cannot resolve two entirely legitimate, but conflicting sentiments.

At the same time, I think that by focusing on Bill you have missed the point. The real issue between us, as I suggested last summer, is the change I underwent when you were in London. I realized that your departures were exhausting me by leaving me with too much responsibility. In my twenties, this made me feel capable. Now that I'm in my thirties, it just tires me out and makes me wonder why I have to take on everything, with no help from you.

That's what needs sorting out. But by walking out over the Bill issue, instead of confronting a situation I assumed we could resolve, you have repeated your pattern—this time leaving me when I don't have the strength to handle the usual responsibilities.

I'm also angry because you expect things to stay the same here, while you live in New York and take on a new lifestyle as casually as you would try out a new pen. This puts me in the very mood that made me vulnerable to Bill. I am not and never was in love with Bill—but while you were away he gave me the attention I HAVE ALWAYS SOUGHT FROM YOU FIRST.

The only reason I did not tell you about what happened on my birthday is that I thought it would hurt you unnecessarily. I feel that you should understand this and should stop punishing me for a situation which, to some extent, was of your making.

I've suffered enough and have made it clear that I want to work on our marriage. You're the man I want, you're the man I need, and you're the man I'm attracted to. Any literary or behavioral references to the albatross (as in your last letter) are artful, but unkind and inappropriate: *I* mate for life. No male albatross worth his feathers would have left me.

Kate

P.S. Please give Peter my love and best wishes for a speedy recovery.

Vesuvio in eruzione
Der Vesuvio in Tatigkeit
Vesuvius in eruption
Vesuve en éruption

10/12/83

Dear Bill – I'm sorry Eros and Sophia are out of whack,* but I'm not good company these days. I cannot help you and it would not help *me* to see you.

And please stop alerting me of Susan Fleet's whereabouts. Seems she always is where Michael's just been – Cornwall, this time. Those spirals of distrust (and unemployment) got me into trouble.

Regards, Kate

P.S. A haunting place, this Herculaneum.

*Have you ever written a letter that did *not* contain a quotation!?

Per Via Area

Professor Bill Stern
Philosophy Hall
Columbia University
New York, New York
10027
U.S.A.

PLEASANTVILLE ELEMENTARY SCHOOL
First Quarter Report

October 28, 1983

Dear Mrs. Hammond,

In all my years of teaching, I have never seen two children at each other's throats more than Judson and Stu Bush. I am not supposed to have favorites, but I must confess that I am extremely fond of both of them. Stu is a quiet, clever rascal, who manages to rile Judson up. But he has a good heart. I have a soft spot for Stu because he is adopted and had to stay back a year because of an eye operation, which set him back as our best reader. Judson is an adorable, brilliant boy, who punches anything or anyone in his path. He is also the laziest speller I have ever come across.

I normally do not get involved with parents unless there is a real problem, but I thought I would tell you about a fantastic thing that happened this week. Judson and Stu volunteered for Show and Tell. For days I could not keep them away from our research library, or from the rubber cement in our supply cabinet. When, at 2:30 yesterday, the time came to reveal what they had, they unrolled a collage featuring every tribal bosom known to National Geographic readers for the past 20 years.

There are moments in teaching where one tries to reprimand, but where one is clearly disposed to laughter. I put the collage away, called Hannah (our

Chorus teacher) and, after she arrived, ran into the teachers lounge and laughed until I cried. Mr. Fishman, the only other teacher there, quieted me down long enough to tell me Judson's Dixie cup story, which set us off again.

The 3:00 bell rang. I rushed back to class, dismissed Hannah, and thanked Judson and Stu for their presentation. I asked them to try and return some of the pictures they had cut out of the magazines; they left gaping holes in all those National Geographics. They were very cooperative.

Maybe their historic rivalry is over.

Regards, Joan Robinson

Pawlet, Vermont

October 29, 1983

Dear Kate,

Your gift arrived today.* Margaret Potter, the 92-year-old dairy maid down the road, has been trying to get me to buy a red tie for years! Margaret insists she can see the color(s) of people's auras. I once made the mistake of calling the town treasurer a bore—"Oh no!" she chirped. "It's just that he's a *latent plaid.*" Curiouser and curiouser. "And what am I?" "A tweed," she replied. (The tie will match my aura—thanks!)

Wish I were as intuitive about relationships as Margaret is about color. I know Michael was upset about you and Bill (don't blame him). But, to some extent, he brought it on himself. What worries me is that he moved out. Seems every time there's a snag between you two, or an inconvenience to his writing schedule, he walks away. But I don't know him as well as I know you (you're the closest anyone's gotten to him), so I hate to judge. If I had met him *before* he came to Columbia—say when he was finishing his research at Harvard, I'd have more to go on. The only thing Dick Bernstein, my colleague from Harvard (remember Michael's dissertation advisor?) used to say about him was that he would do *anything* to avoid disagreements with people, especially women, and that he *never* got his work in on time. But Michael's 44 years old now, so I doubt this information is of use to a woman who has been his wife for 14 years!

I feel for you "young" couples. In my day, things were never as complicated. When I went to Oxford in 1938 for a year's research, Jane came with me. None of this you-go-your-way-I'll-go-mine: people stuck together—even when they shouldn't have.

I'm *not* suggesting that you should give up your work or that Michael should give up writing. But, since your role has changed over the course of the marriage (you're no longer his student), you'll both have to be flexible to make it work—*very* flexible. I know *you* are. I'm not sure *he* is—but, as I've said, I don't know him well enough.

Tell you what I do know. Michael's a writer. And not just any kind of writer—he's a poet. The thing about poets is that they will seek any set of circumstances that allows them to do their best work. Some need a quiet home life that places no demands upon them; others look to booze, women/men, and other sources of inspiration. When I say Inspiration, I'm not talking about the nineteenth century Romantic notion of some idiot listening to birds. Nor do I refer to the myth that poets have to get smashed before they can write a decent line.** I am talking about the fact that poets are like listening posts, of a sensory nature. And they won't put up with any static that might interfere with their apprehension of an image, a sound, or an emotion.

When I first introduced you two, I had no idea that Michael was more than, potentially, one of our best English professors (he had yet to publish his first book of poetry). Two volumes later, I'm convinced that he's not just a poet, he's a *fine* one. THIS DOES NOT MEAN THAT YOU SHOULD PUT UP WITH HIM. It means that, throughout the years, his commitment has deepened, just as yours has.

De tout mon coeur, Robert.
Love to Judson and Scrunch!

* You needn't always follow your visits with a present!
** Though I never met a poet who wasn't a bit of a boozehound.

Inwood Road
Pleasantville, New York

November 6, 1983

Dear Robert,

Thanks for your wisdom. I'll tell you what's frustrating me: I care very much about my work, but I care more about my marriage. So when I see Michael move out because he happens to be hurt, happens to want more time to write, happens to want to be closer to Columbia, and happens to have inherited a sum from his former landlady in London that helps him afford his apartment in New York, I think—how much can Michael really care about our marriage?

Maybe I know the answer. But what makes me the one who is constantly trying to rescue things?

Love,
Kate

300 Riverside Drive
New York City

November 8, 1983

Darling–

Does it comfort you to know that I regard this move as temporary? I need some time away–I guess London was only the first indication. If my behavior repeats a pattern that has become unacceptable to you, then it confirms my sense that you, not I, have changed during the course of our marriage. It makes me sad to say this, but I think you will continue to grow–probably away from me.

When I am honest with myself, I admit that my decision to move had *very little* to do with what happened between you and Bill. That's not to say it didn't leave a scar, but it does mean that I really don't hold it against you. If I did I would be a hypocrite. I've done a few things I'm not proud of.

I wish I could give you answers to all the questions you raise, but I cannot. And, ultimately, there might not be any–certainly not any that would satisfy you. You're right about one thing: I would like things to stay the same while I'm away. But I am realistic enough not to expect them to–if only because you move more quickly than I do and, once you have sorted things out, you'll probably decide that I'm no good. Then you'll move on and, most likely, not look back.

This is the best I can do. As you know (to your great frustration), I am not articulate about my feelings. I suppose many men are like me: the worst of us drift, the best of us simply plod on. I'm sure it's no excuse, but you should know that this pathetic behavior has nothing to do with not caring or not feeling. I guess we bruise internally.

My book comes out in the spring and I'm finding some satisfaction in my work. Turns out Peter's workshop students are exceptional writers. They mastered the sestina I assigned, so I'll stop measuring their poems by the foot.

In today's class, one woman's poem, "Convertible," provoked a lively discussion on the subject of aural precision. One man said he had trouble with the line—"Driving fast— / to spank my face against the wind / and suffocate." He could not hear the "spank." Another woman defended Alicia's word choice: You don't have to hear the spanking sound, she said, you have to feel the spanking action of the wind against the narrator's face. "Hands up if you think Alicia gets away with it," I said. Results: 10 to 2 in her favor. Getting away with it, I suggested, is what it's all about.

The only other objection was raised by a convertible owner who insisted that there was no way the '67 Rambler Alicia referred to in the poem could be a convertible. "Well, was it?" another verification specialist asked. Alicia stunned the class by saying, "I don't know, I've never been in a convertible." Well, then how can you write about them, asked our car expert; whereupon Alicia said, "I make stuff up all the time." "Is that proper?" asked the youngest member of the class. I told them I had once written a poem about manatees and had never seen a manatee (didn't tell them you were my eyes). A few looked at me with revulsion. Poets make stuff up all the time, I said.

May I come see you and the children this weekend?

All my love, Michael

Inwood Road
Pleasantville, New York

November 15, 1983

Dearest Michael,

Every time you are honest about your feelings, as you were in your last letter, you give me hope that we can work things out—so please stop anticipating any future actions on my part. I am still committed to our marriage.

Just after you called and asked about coming this weekend, Elaine rang to invite us for Thanksgiving. Why don't you come then, instead? I'll be done with Herculaneum and might have time to pick you up and drop off the trunk you left in the basement.

You're missing some terrific domestic events. Today one of Dr. Nelson's grandsons darted under our hedge and pulled his pants down in front of Elaine's daughter Terry. "PUT THAT THING AWAY," Terry yelled, pointing at his thing, "I've seen 'em a thousand times!"

Judson and Jeanne have been asking biological questions ever since.

Kate

Inwood Road
Pleasantville, New York

November 15, 1983

Dear Daddy,

I'm going to be 12 on November 24 (don't forget), but that is not why I am writing this letter. I have been reading some of the books you left in the basement. Most of them were in the trunk. So far I finished *Tess* by Thomas Hardy. Next I will read *Forbidden Games* by a French man.

Then I will read *Green Mansions* by W. H. Hudson, but I did not want to tell Mom because on the inside it says To My Dearest Susan. And twice I heard Mom talking once to Grandma and once to Elaine saying that bitch Susan. So I wanted to tell you without telling her, even though I am very scared of telling anybody.

Judson and I miss you very much and wish you and Mommy would get back together. Sometimes it hurts so much Judson and I just look at each other and try not to get very upset. We wish it would all go away.

But we love you and wish we could see you more than sometimes on weekends.

xxxxxxxxxxxScrunch

300 Riverside Drive
New York City

November 19, 1983

Honey—

Daddy loves *you,* loves *Mommy,* loves *Judson* VERY MUCH.

See you on your birthday!

X X X X X

HUNTER, STEIN
14 Irving Place
New York City

November 23, 1983

Dear Michael,

When you called and said you probably wouldn't make your December 1 deadline, you sounded a bit harried. I just want to assure you that the *worst* thing that can happen is a later publication date.

If you want the book to appear by the end of June (which, I think, is to your advantage, unless you are prepared to wait until September), I must have the manuscript by December 31st. We'll have to turn it around very quickly, more quickly than I like to—but I leave it up to you.

Best,
George Stein

Pawlet, Vermont

November 26, 1983

Dear Michael,

I'm glad you called. Based on what you've said, I think you've got to come clean. Doesn't matter that Susan is no longer the issue. Ten years ago she *was* and, most important, you've been dishonest this past year by pretending not to know her.

I shuddered when you said, "I hoped it would go away if I just let it run its course." One thing I have learned is that, however much you wish they would, PEOPLE DON'T JUST DISAPPEAR BECAUSE YOU WILL THEM OUT OF YOUR LIFE. If anything, they tend to converge. The fact that Susan popped up in London (I *do* believe you had no idea she'd be there) proves my point.

Don't know if Kate will buy your reasons for not telling her. But I can assure you that whether you, or Scrunch, or Bill (who must be on to something), or Susan, or I tell her—it *will* come out.

I'm so discouraged about you and Kate I almost wish I had never introduced you.

Robert

Second Semester

But once he knew my welcome, I alone
Could give him subtle increase and reflection.
Seamus Heaney, "*Undine*"

Bronxville, New York

January 2, 1984

Sweetheart—

I cannot endure another Christmas and New Year's like this last one. Despite your optimism and efforts to keep everyone happy, the pain was palpable. I asked Santa point blank why he had moved out and—goddamn that incommunicative sonofabitch—he just looked at me with his big brown eyes and said, "I wonder if it's the appropriate time to discuss this." I'm sure you fell for those eyes 15 years ago. Well, as far as I am concerned, 15 years later, his eyes are his *only* attraction. Never mind his height, never mind his physique, never mind his pretty words. Fact is that, for all his sentimentality and sensitivity, he does exactly what he wants. I know you love him, but I cannot find excuses for him anymore. He's lost his innocence because every time you ask him for answers he does not respond—for whatever reasons—laziness, indifference, or some genetic incapacity.

He's decisive only when he's making one of his great escapes and, this last one, his move to New York, was a little too dramatic for my taste in a son-in-law. He cannot be punishing you for one night's sin with Bill, so I hope you've stopped blaming yourself for that. I never thought I would say things like this but, frankly, under the circumstances, *I think it was the most intelligent thing you've done in years* (besides Herculaneum, which was on television last night).

I don't trust Michael because he moves like the carp in our pond out back. And his talk is cheap, even if it *is* poetry. Sometimes I think you'd have been better off with a fireman. Would have told you this over the phone, but you'd have hung up on me.

Love, Mom

P.S. If worse comes to worst, we'll deal with it. Hold on to your work.

300 Riverside Drive
New York City

January 6, 1984

Dear George,

This is to confirm what we already discussed today by phone. Having missed my December 31 deadline, I agree to submit *Green Park* (is the title still negotiable?) no later than March 31, thereby assuring publication for September.

(Will this do for your lawyers?)

Sorry about this. You've been very patient.
I'm feeling tired and empty.

Best, Michael

45 West 89th Street
New York, New York

January 10, 1984

Dear Michael Hammond,

You have many former students, so you might not remember me. I'm the one who wrote about things I had never experienced—convertibles, bell-ringing, and the Taj Mahal.

Your workshop was very important to me. It was the first time I had showed my poems to anybody. I am writing because I would like to know if you will be offering it again. I work for a lawyer during the day, so the General Studies course is, unfortunately, the only one I can take.

I still find time to write—usually before work, then a quick look at my morning's work at lunch, followed by a stiff edit in the evening after returning from dinner.

I enclose my "Crow," a *real* one!, which, for reasons I do not understand, hatched on Superbowl Sunday. Please do not feel that you have to comment.

Regards,
Alicia Price

Crow

Nervous bird–
jet plumes flattened to a seal shine.

Marauder–
stop needling my garden.

You've no place
among my crab apple pinks,
marbled tulips, trumpet vines.

Already I've had to
kitchen-twine the lilacs,
hell-bent on smothering you.

Greaser–
the closest thing to vinyl
God allowed in the garden.

CURIOSITY
Gerard Ter Borch (1617–1681)
Oil on Canvas, 76,3/62,3 cm
The Metropolitan Museum of Art. New York
The Jules Bache Collection, 1949

1/15/84

Dear Alicia,

I'm teaching an advanced workshop this semester. I've asked students to submit samples of their work, but with your "Crow" you've satisfied all requirements.

First class is February 5th, so you might want to sign up soon.

See you in class.

Michael Hammond

Alicia Price
45 West 89th Street
New York, New York
10024

COLUMBIA UNIVERSITY

Philosophy Hall

January 16, 1984

Dear Kate,

WAIT! Before you put this in your Bill Stern Letter Shredding Machine, I want to bring you news that, I think, will make you happy. Susan Fleet is marrying an investment banker. I had dinner with her and Norman last night (she wanted my opinion) and have concluded that they're a good match. I drilled him as best I could, considering I know very little about his work. All I could make out was that he always seems to be in the trendiest areas of banking. At Mortebank and Co., he started with syndicated loans to Latin America, then went on to Eurobonds, followed by mergers and acquisitions and, now, it's leveraged buyouts.

Susan's marriage marks the loss of a third friend this year. You were the first—Michael, the second. Though I am more rational than intuitive, I sense that Michael knows what happened. Last term I tried to engage him in a conversation about freedom of expression with the Dean of our law school. But he showed little interest and, in general, avoids me on campus. Under normal circumstances The Motherfucker Trilogy—Rosenfeld, Lewis and Brown, all in 1972—would have been a subject of great amusement to Michael. Rosenfeld used "mother fucking" on four occasions to describe the teachers, the school board, the town, and his own country when addressing a school board meeting in New Jersey. Lewis called the police officer who was arresting her son "a goddamn mother fucker," and Brown, in a meeting in a university chapel, referred to some policemen as "mother fucker fascist pig cops." Well, I imagine it's you who are most interested in the First Amendment from a professional point of view. And I guess a poem would collapse under the weight of so much cursing, which is why Michael might have rejected "fighting words" as suitable material for his work.

What I am saying, really, is that I was trying to be friendly and helpful because without Michael and the rest of you to count among my friends, I feel like a leper. In fact, I even thought about teaching a course called "The Leper Colony as a Philosophical Paradigm." I'm better now, but this year has been one of those character-building years I can do without.

Hope you, Michael, and the children are well and happy,

Bill

P.S. Hilda, an officious *apparatchik* in the English Department, told me that Michael had moved out on you. I told her to lay off the herbal cigarettes and advised her not to spread rumors!

Inwood Road
Pleasantville, New York

January 18, 1984

Dear Mom,

Thanks for your letter, but I'm not ready to hear that kind of harangue against someone who is still my husband. The marriage is worth saving. It's like what Franklin Delano Roosevelt said about Somoza: "He may be a sonofabitch, but he's *our* sonofabitch."

Love, Kate

45 West 89th Street
New York, New York

February 10, 1984

Dear Michael,

I enclose a poem I started last semester and have recently revised. Your comments, as always, would be appreciated. It's my turn to read this week but, instead of showing the class "Spring Carnage" (I junked "Convertible" as a title), I'd rather show them a new poem.

Regards,
Alicia

P.S. Show me your poems.

Spring Carnage

I understand
why one mad fly
spat against the bulb last night
and fried alive.

I would do it another way—
in a sun-dappled convertible,
driving fast, to
spank my face against the wind
and suffocate.

Or else I'd be the murderess—
cupping and plucking scarlet tulips
(well-versed in cognac goblets)
and steal away when all, en masse,
mouthe riot on my calves!

Come June
the spring air thickens
(sun-butter melting in)
and I who am Furious
die—Embalmed
in chokes of pert mosquitoes.

300 Riverside Drive
New York City

February 14, 1984

Dearest Kate,

Sometimes I think we might try living in New York. Your work is here and so is mine. We could take summers in the country, rent houses in Europe—whatever. Just a Valentine's Day nightdream?

Had my picture taken today for the back cover of my book. Wore the Kate's-eye green sweater you gave me for Christmas, only to be told that the photo's black and white.

Spent the better part of class assuring my workshop students that *plume* and *noon* do not rhyme. Sometimes, for an advanced workshop, these students surprise me at-once with their talent and ignorance. Only Alicia (the one who makes stuff up) picked up on it. She brought in Cupid lollipops for everyone, today, which may have affected their judgment.

Peter Clare is very much on my mind. The doctors at Mt. Sinai have been poking around and taking pictures of his insides; the latest word is that they think he has cancer. Doesn't seem fair. He never smoked or drank—his only passions were Cathy, his teaching, and his poetry, which he refuses to publish.

This letter's a bit aimless because I am not writing about what I intended to discuss with you.

Should that wait for the next time I see you? Don't seem to be able to finish my book—*my* Ides of March falls on the 31st.

May I come up next weekend?

All my love, Michael

FLAYING OF MARSYAS
Titian (c 1488–1576)
This horrific scene from classical mythology depicts the satyr Marsyas being flayed alive by Apollo. Marsyas had challenged the god Apollo to a contest of musical skill and lost. Here, Apollo and his Phrygian assistant, peel away Marsyas' skin with careful attention.

Pawlet,
2/16/84

Well?

Robert

Michael Hammond
300 Riverside Drive
New York, New York
10025

Inwood Road
Pleasantville, New York

February 21, 1984

Dear Michael,

I know you were just "nightdreaming," but it had crossed my mind to move into the city with you. The more I thought about it, the more I remembered one aspect of my childhood I did not want Judson and Jeanne to experience.

Where I grew up, no one had a sense of place. No one had childhood stories to tell and those who did didn't value their significance. Out There was where things were happening, especially for adults who worked in the city.

I don't want the children to go through this emotional shiftlessness. Right now, they *don't* have the displaced sense that everything is happening elsewhere, somewhere after the commute. And I think it's because we live in a neighborhood—a real one, one I never had.

I'm sorry about your students' alternative displays of stupidity and brilliance—even *I* knew *plume* and *noon* did not rhyme.

I'm sorriest of all to hear about Peter.

And whatever it is you want to talk about, I'm here.

Love, Kate

P.S. *Finish* your book!

45 West 89th Street
New York, New York

February 24, 1984

Dear Michael,

Forgive me for being so impetuous, but here's another one I hope you have time to look at before our next class.

Alicia

P.S. Your poem, "The Homecoming," was beautiful.

Separation

Hurricane Ridge
Washington

Can you see the way
the wildflowers stipple
the bank of that stream,
Or notice how the mountain's
snow and chocolate,
like a cow's flank?

We are climbing over splinters
from a long-departed glacier—
Where has all the driftwood come from?
The sun has baked its veins
and glazed it silver!

For hours I have breathed
the dust your boots have lifted.
For just as long I have trained my eyes
on your generalissimo's *ass for direction.*
My ears are ringing with stories of your failed marriage.
And amidst the paraphernalia of sun visors,
glacier glasses, day packs and walking sticks,
I will remember this day
for what wanted to happen.

Instead, we drank beer
at the Dungeness Tavern
and watched billiard balls pocket
with a burnished snap.

Dinner that night
was steamed clams, clam nectar;
not you.

Inwood Road
Pleasantville, New York

February 28, 1984

Dear Daddy,

Today Miss Hans taught me C minor. I already know my major scales. Then I tried to stretch my hand an octave, but was still 3 keys short. I love Miss Hans. She gave me a beautiful piece called "The Girl with the Flaxen Hair" by Debussy because she says it reminds her of me. If I learn that, she promised to let me play "Gertrude's Dream Waltz" by Beethoven. I fell in love with it when Miss Hans played it for me.

Mrs. Letucci still lets me practice as much as I want on her piano. She is very nice because most of the time I have to play a piece many times before I get it right.

Mom says we are probably going to North Carolina again this year for our Spring vacation!!!!!!!! Are you coming with us??????

PLEASE?

Love, Jeanne

WALTER FEINSTEIN, D.D.S.
30 Rockefeller Plaza
New York, New York 10020

March 1, 1984

Dear Michael,

I have thought about this a great deal and have come to the conclusion that it is perhaps time for you to find a new dentist. I can no longer in good faith work on your teeth without feeling that I would be doing your wife and children a better service if I were to attempt to drill through your bridge to China.

What goes on between you and Kate is your business. However, I have seen her sad for many months. Elaine spends a great deal of time with your children and she says they are not as happy as usual.

Elaine and I know very little about poetry. We have no doubts about your being a fine professor and an excellent writer. I have tremendous problems with your values as a man, however. If Kate is not the most important person or thing in your life, then I truly believe that you are very weak or very stupid or both. I feel very unkind as I write this but I also feel very strongly.

Sincerely, Walter

P.S. Please do not feel that you have to pay the invoice from your last visit. And I am recommending that you use the services of Irving Gorenstein, D.D.S., who is probably a better dentist than me.

Inwood Road
Pleasantville, New York

March 5, 1984

Dear Robert,

Relapse. I'm losing it. Am trying to sort out my feelings and those of Michael at the same time. I know what's bothering me, but I don't know what, if anything, is eating at him. He won't talk and I can't stand the wait.

I know he loves me, but that doesn't seem to make things work. I miss him. Can't stop picturing the predatory curve of his back as he goes after one of his poems with a Bic Medium Black.

The kids don't understand any more than I do. And they miss him terribly. How is it that Michael's passivity is so cruel!? He's been saying, lately, that he wants to talk—then never does. If I call and try to draw him out, he just says that he misses us all, very much.

For the first time, I get a frightening, swooning feeling when I think about our marriage. It's the same swirl and drop I used to feel when I was a child before falling into a sleep I thought I'd never be able to come out of. No appetite, either. And I'm having trouble concentrating on my next film.

I wish I could remember whether these problems existed before I talked to Michael about my changes. Or did I destroy my marriage by opening my mouth!? Jesus, was our marriage THAT fragile?

When I talk with Michael about my fears, he just holds me. Yet his affection doesn't console me—I worry that every time we're together it might be our last.

I want all this pain to go away.

All my love, Kate

45 West 89th Street
New York, New York

March 8, 1984

Dear Michael,

You are always telling me that my meter is irregular, so I thought I would study up on meter, rhyme, and blank verse.

Came across this sonnet by John Updike which, I thought, might make you smile. Though a conventional English sonnet in form, it violates all conventions of delicacy and reduces sex to an onomatopoetic pursuit!

Love Sonnet

In Love's rubber armor I come to you,
b
oo
b.
c,
d
c
d:
e
f—
e
f.
g
g.

XX Alicia

P.S. If you are married, please put your ring on to dash my hopes (and I'll no more of this).

COLUMBIA UNIVERSITY
Department of English

Lewisohn—Room 408

Friday, March 10, 1984

Bill—

Please let me know if you're free for a drink to-morrow evening.

Michael

300 Riverside Drive
New York City

Sunday, March 12, 1984

Dearest Kate,

Please call off your dogs. Walter's taken me off his patient list, Robert's affection for me has chilled, you've kept me at bay this weekend, and my children have stopped writing. I can't be all that bad—Bill doesn't think so. We had drinks last night and, after 5 whiskeys, even the Pope would have forgiven Bill (as I did) for his mortal sin.

He's loyal—and looked very sad when I told him that I had taken an apartment in New York. "If you and Kate have problems," he said, "then I've lost all faith in marriage as an institution." He mentioned Susan Fleet's engagement to Norman Solomon and the news so relieved us both that we toasted Norm, then quite spontaneously broke into Robert Service's ballad:

M—"A bunch of boys were whooping it up in the Malamute saloon."

(with Bill drawing strength and audibility toward the middle . . .)

B—"That someone had stolen the woman you loved; that her love was a devil's lie;
That your guts were gone, and the best for you was to crawl away and die."

Poor Bill. Do we have anybody for him?

And you, my lionhearted Kate, will you please let me come home on weekends?

M.

COLUMBIA UNIVERSITY

Philosophy Hall

Sunday, March 12

Dear Kate,

I have a vague memory of the first completely worthless evening of my life. I think it was good for me. I happen to have spent it with your husband, who is just as worthless as me, but no more worthless than most men. I swear to *God* this time, never mind Nietzsche; I don't understand why women put up with such worthlessness, even when each worthless moment is spent in worthless rumination about the gender they infuriate most—women.

Michael talked about you the whole time. He kept on saying he was no good, and would not say why. I agreed with him. You *are* worthless, I said. How the hell could you leave your wife and kids to finish a lousy book of poems? And when you *didn't* finish, how could you move out on her *again,* to finish the *same* lousy book of poems? He swore on a stack of bibles that he had wanted you to come to London with the children—said you had planned it that way, but that it had not worked out. As for the move, he insisted it was temporary.

I had to stop there because, *just* when I had him pinned against the wall, Michael said, "We won't go into it—*but you're pretty fucking worthless yourself!*" (I had to agree.)

I take full responsibility for the way the discussion degenerated. I asked him to recall the first words that had ever caught his ear. For me, it was Lewis Carroll's "Jabberwocky." Michael's earliest aural memories were the noisy verses his father had picked up in army intelligence camp; the following verse had to be translated into 25 languages. I found it scribbled on my cocktail napkin this morning.

Here, then, with Michael's recitation, is how our worthless evening ended:

The sexual life of the camel
is stranger than anyone thinks.
One night in a deep fit of passion,
he endeavored to bugger the sphinx.
But the sphinx's posterior portions
are blocked by the sands of the Nile,
which accounts for the hump on the camel
*and the sphinx's inscrutable smile.**

Love,
Bill (sober as a judge)

* Apologies for yet another quotation.

300 Riverside Drive
New York City

March 17, 1984

Dear Kate,

Thanks to you, I am witnessing the mass intimacy of a New York Sunday. In the window opposite mine, a woman is washing her lover's back and, just now, another couple has started the same pre-brunch ablutions. Funny how New York so unsentimentally robs unwitting people of their souls. Mine's still intact, but if you keep on refusing to let me come home on weekends, I might (God forbid) turn into one of these faceless lovers.

I'm planning to visit Peter this afternoon. But first I promised Dorothy Cross, the publicist at Hunter, Stein, an invitations list. The party's not until September, but she has managed to convince me that *her* list is more important than *my* poems (just about done)! She has asked for 100 names to fill the dining hall at the Poetry Society, but I cannot come up with even half that many. Especially after I subtract our "mutual" friends who, given the slightest opportunity to show their allegiance, disappear from my social register.

I'm tired of spending my Sundays with Ulysses S. Grant on the Upper West Side. Makes me feel like a pigeon.

And what's all this nonsense about a family vacation without Dad?

Love to you, Judson, and Jeanne,
M.

300 Riverside Drive
New York City

March 21, 1984

Darling–

2:54 AM. Book *done*. Last poem closed itself with a rapid burst, then a shutting, much like a snap-dragon in the palm.

All my love,
M.

Inwood Road
Pleasantville, New York

April 2, 1984

Dear M–

Been very busy trying to shoot an hour on a rock star called Zorba. Her seismic voice almost blew my soundman's ears. Her dancing almost cost me a cameraman–she shimmied up to Ed, then spun around and stalked down the audience like some Jezebel in toreador pants. I knew what I was in for even before I started shooting. Her coiffure, resembling electrified straw, suggested that she had a direct line to some previously untapped energy source.

YES, I am, quite possibly, taking Judson and Jeanne to North Carolina. Thought of you, yesterday, as I stood on that damn trunk of books in the basement. Was trying to screw in a lightbulb–not tall enough. Judson's old fish tank and Jeanne's box of dolls came tumbling down.

That lightbulb–along with the lawn, a pile of laundry high as Mont Blanc, and windows that make me wonder if I have cataracts, will all be here for you while I'm away.* Surprise me. Make them all disappear.

Kate

P.S. I'm *very* happy you finished your book.

* Also–to follow–the information you will need to complete this year's taxes.

300 Riverside Drive
New York City

April 18, 1984

Dear Kate,

Tried calling. Guess you really did leave without me.

Peter's not well. He was ill in England. Feel like a fool. Wish I had been told. Only Cathy knew.

I think he's going to die. Setting those words down makes me confront their incontrovertibility.

I miss you.

Michael

Nags Head, North Carolina

April 21, 1984

Dear Dad!

Guess what? My friend Skip is back this year and he gave me a fishing rod! Thank you for the Echaskech. I would like a new baseball mit (a ketchers mit) for my birthday. I got into trouble in school again before I left but I dont think Mr. Fishman will tell on me.

This time when we came down we followed all the gull signs to the Chessapeek Tunnel that almost never ends!

Why didn't you come?

Love your son,
Judson

LES SABINES
Jacques Louis David (1748–1825)
Paris—Musée du Louvre

4/22/84

M—
Thanks for dinner

(I'm in love with you).

A.

Michael Hammond
300 Riverside Drive
New York, New York
10025

Nags Head, North Carolina

April 23, 1984

Dear Daddy,

Judson and I stared at jet trails in the sky today because we liked the way it looked like the Etch-a-Sketch you bought us. We use it a lot.

Mom takes us for long walks on the beach. She always wants to go at least as far as the lighthouse, but Judson and I can barely make it to the pier. Mack asks about you and so does Hazel.

I have not told anybody about the books. When Mom asked to see the *Green Mansions* I brought down I told her I wasn't done with it so she did not look.

Judson fishes with Skip a lot because Skip is back this year and gave Judson the fishing rod his son Chuck left when he went to Annapolis.

I made a friend Careen. She has the blackest face I have ever seen and the whitest smile. She swims better than all the boys in the pool and is teaching me how to dive like a jacknife when the boys aren't doing cannonballs.

I wish you were here very much.

Love, Jeanne

P.S. We took the Chesapeake Bay Tunnel this time to get here!

Nags Head, North Carolina

April 26, 1984

Dear Robert,

All this beauty, but nothing compelling about it, nothing to draw me towards it without the person who makes me feel it most intensely. Left Michael in New York because I'm drained—from work and because of Michael. I don't feel we're getting anywhere. Vacation wouldn't have solved anything. We'd have had a great time, then he'd have gone back to his apartment. At this point, I want him all the time, or not at all. Still, each time the lighthouse blinks, I feel he's watching me—a flood of white light, if only for a nanosecond.

How long will it take, I WANT TO KNOW, for things to resolve—one way or another, I *want* a resolution.

Hope you are well and happy,

Love, Kate

45 West 89th Street
New York, New York

April 27, 1984

Dear Michael,

I never studied with Peter, but most of the workshop students did. I wish I could help them, I wish I could help you, I wish I could help Peter.

If you'd like me to go with you when you visit him today (or any day)—even if it's just to wait for you outside the hospital (it might not be appropriate for me to go up), I *will*.

You were very sweet to be concerned about me last night, but please don't be. I'm the least of your worries. And even if you go back to Kate, I'll understand. I never expected as much as I've had already.

Love, Alicia

ACADEMY OF TELEVISION ARTS
AND SCIENCES

May 9, 1984

Dear Kate Hammond,

It is our pleasure to inform you that your one-hour program, "Manatee," has been nominated for an Emmy Award in the Children's Program category. The awards ceremony will be held on Friday, July 14, in the Grand Ballroom of the New York Hilton.

We look forward to seeing you there.

Regards,
Ruth Mitchell
Awards Manager

Pleasantville, New York
Inwood Road

8 PM

May 11, 1984

Dear Michael,

Tried calling you. You're never in. Jeanne's piano teacher just called to say that, for the past five months, Jeanne has not snapped out of crying spells at most of her lessons. When asked what the matter is, she keeps telling Miss Hans, "It's a secret."

I know Jeanne and Judson want to see us back together—*that's no secret,* to you or to me. Is there anything I should know that Jeanne has told you and is keeping from me?

If so, I *want* to know. I'm worried.

Kate

P.S. Will be in New York this week attending ballet rehearsals at Lincoln Center (possible ballet film for Adele)—but, *most important,* to see Peter.

Inwood Road
Pleasantville, New York

May 14, 1984

Dear M—

Thought you should see this letter from Judson's science teacher. I'll be out of town this week and would appreciate your taking care of it.

Thanks and XXKate

P.S. I forgot to tell you I've been nominated for an Emmy.

PLEASANTVILLE ELEMENTARY SCHOOL
Mr. John Fishman

Dear Mrs. Hammond,

To some extent I am honored that my teachings in science over the past three years have inspired Judson to experiment with suction, dissection, and, most recently, solar energy.

Today Judson's curiosity went too far, however, and had it gone unchecked, Judson might have endangered his fellow students. During recess, he aimed a magnifying glass at a leaf and started a fire that a few students were eager to fuel with their third quarter report cards. Out of vanity, Judson spared his own report card but, without hesitation, accepted those of the three slowest students in the class (each had an F or two to turn into ashes).

Judson promised he would not repeat the experiment and I believe him. My hunch is that he'll try out another one instead. In the meantime, I live in fear.

Judson is a fine boy, but, I think you will understand, I have to take disciplinary measures. I am making him prepare a five-minute talk on the Pleasantville Fire Department. If either you or Mr. Hammond would assist me by taking Judson on a brief tour of the facility (they are very nice and I have sent them budding pyromaniacs before), I would appreciate it.

I am sorry to inconvenience you.

Regards, John Fishman

CHILDREN'S TELEVISION NETWORK

New York, New York

May 15, 1984

Dear Kate,

A brief note to tell you how proud we are for your Emmy Award nomination! We're convinced you're going to win and the Art Department has already designed the T-shirts for our one-week fund-raising drive (which will feature your film):

KEEP MANATEES WHERE THEY BELONG—
ON THE AIR!

If Metrovision hasn't snatched you up for their Rockvision special, we would like you to consider doing the three-hour series I mentioned on ballet schools all over the world.

Congratulations and let me know if you are interested in our project.

Adele Harris

COLUMBIA UNIVERSITY

Philosophy Hall

May 20, 1984

Dear Kate,

Don't ask me why, but I find myself wanting very much to keep you and Michael together. If you knew how much he loves you, if you had seen him yesterday, as I did, speak at Peter Clare's funeral service. Everything he was saying convinced me that you two belong together.

As you have probably heard, Peter was a kind man and one of our best professors. He was also a poet at heart. In the Poet's Corner of St. John the Divine, Michael told some 300 people that Peter would *not* be immortalized here, but he *should* have been, so great was his commitment to the teaching and the practice of poetry.

Michael addressed Peter's wife, Cathy, and her seven-year-old son, saying how much he would miss Peter. And as only Michael can, he spun in two phrases that haunted us all—repeating each one at the end of some moving remembrance: "Death is the mother of beauty" (Wallace Stevens), and he ended with Simon Weil's "Distance is the soul of beauty." Of course, we were all reduced to tears.

The minister gave a marvelous eulogy about Peter's new life with God, but, as Michael said after it was over, "I just wish I could believe it." My only hope is that Peter's beautiful wife, herself only 29, *did* believe it.

I have been thinking about you and Michael a lot, probably because Michael and I are now good friends, and one thing that strikes me is that he continues to do the only two things he knows how to do—teach and write poetry. With other men, take Norman (Susan's husband), the only thing they know how to do is to make money. But it's really the same point: Norman has told me that he feels a bit insecure sometimes because the only things he has to offer Susan are love and financial security. In Michael's case, I think he worries that all he can give you are pretty words and a very difficult love. Whatever his faults, he is, in his own way, passionate about you.

The whole thing makes me feel so sad and is so against all logic that I can't stand it!

Love,
Bill

45 West 89th Street
New York, New York

May 21, 1984

Dear Michael,

What you said about Peter robbed *Revelation* (XXI) of its gems!

I could almost see him, key in hand—*he got in!*

All my love,
Alicia

Pawlet, Vermont

May 25, 1984

Dear Kate,

Belated thanks for your Nags Head missive—been outta town. Happened to be in New York at the time of Peter Clare's funeral. Michael's words sang to the angels. I know what he's putting you through, but that damned rascal could read the list of milking instructions off my barn door and make the cows cry.

This doesn't help you any, so I'll shut up.

Any new developments?

Love, Robert

New York, New York
May 26, 1984

Dear Kate,

Just the kind of note you want to get after you've left the network. Remember Deborah Feder? She is finally taking us to court over your documentary on The Homeless. Took her three years to put the case together, but here it is. She was able to identify her frumpy (but *not homeless*) likeness in the "street" footage you used for the following narration:

> *. . . The lucky few*
> *find food from a soup kitchen . . .*
> *warmth from a subway grille . . .*
>
> *clothes from the refuse of the rich** . . .
> *and bedding from a park bench.*

I could have taken care of this for you, but Peter Burke, our general counsel, is nervous. Ever since the last libel case, he has requested outside counsel on *all* our cases.

Your involvement will be minimal. Expect a call from John VanDine at Mudd, White (nice guy, good lawyer). He'll be representing you.

Sorry about all this. Heard about your Emmy nomination. I knew you'd land on your feet.

Best, Harry Josephson

* Enter, the badly dressed (but *not homeless* Deborah).

300 Riverside Drive
New York City

May 27, 1984

Dearest K–

Had a pleasant chat with Fire Marshall Turnbull to make an appointment for myself and for our son, Prometheus. July 3rd was the soonest they could do it, but they promised it would be the height of the fire season.

I know Jeanne, even more than Judson, has been affected by our split. The best thing is for her father to come home. He wants to, he's ready to, he wonders if he may.

Sorry I've been so elusive. Was spending most of my time with Peter, who, with great beauty and dignity, made dying look easy.

Cathy appreciated your call, your flowers, and your letter. I was sorry you couldn't be there.

It's been very rough not having you this past month.

I'm a bit angry that you took off without me (I needed you).

All my love, Michael

P.S. I'm *proud* of you for the Emmy nomination.

Part Three

NEW YORK

Summer

One moment more, Monsieur Executioner!
Jeanne du Barry

Inwood Road
Pleasantville, New York

July 1, 1984

Dear Robert,

Since you last wrote, I've been seeing a you-know-what. Her name is Bea, and she says I should start writing things down. Only reason I'm going is that Michael caught me by surprise with his offer to come home.

I have doubts about giving money (lots of it) to someone who knows nothing about me and cannot *really* care. But here's what happened; and, even at the risk of burdening you, I *want* you to know what goes on (yours is a healthy skepticism that won't let Bea lead me astray).

First Session

"Do you want him to come home?"

(What a stupid question. You could fit a lifetime between those words.)

"He's stirred up a lot of muck by asking if he can come home."

"Why?"

"Because I'd like to rip his head off first and *then* let him come home."

"You sound angry."

"Just your ordinary love and rage. I'm sure you've seen lots of it."

"What bothers you most?"

"That he left when *he* decided to, that he wants to come home when *he's* ready."

"Anything else?"

"That by asking my permission, he forces *me* to make the decision."

"Do you make most of the decisions?"

"For the household, yes."

"Do you resent making most of the decisions?"

"I hate *doing* everything."

"Like what?"

"Screwing lightbulbs in sockets got me really mad the other day. Everything fell from the shelves and I started to cry."

(I started crying in front of Bea. I couldn't stop.)

"Why did you cry?"

"Because I couldn't *do* it!"

"Lots of people can't reach light sockets."

"I can't do—" (I thought "do" was the longest word in the world.) "I can't do *EVERYTHING!*"

"Why do you try to?"

(Sob, sob, more sobs.) "If I didn't it wouldn't get done."

"What if you didn't do everything and it didn't get done? What's the worst that could happen?"

"He wouldn't lo—"

"Love you?"

(Nod, nod, more nods.) "He wouldn't love me."

Bea said, "Bullshit."

"You're not supposed to do that," I said.

"Do what?"

"You're not supposed to interact. That's what they *say*."

"Who says?"

"People who have done this before."

Bea said, "Bullshit."

And only after she had said "Bullshit" for the second time did I think that we might be able to work together.

Love, Kate

YOUNG GIRL IN BLUE
Amedeo Modigliani (1884–1920)
Private Collection

7/4/84

Dear Alicia,

I think we should avoid any fireworks tonight. I've been feeling this for a while. Seems the appropriate time to tell you.

Hope you don't feel betrayed. I think I've been honest. You've turned my head — I'll never deny that. But my marriage, it seems, has been stretched to a breaking point.

Fondly, Michael

P.S. If I were you, I wouldn't vogue that last poem you sent. You're capable of better work.

Alicia Price
45 West 89th Street
New York, New York
10024

Inwood Road
Pleasantville, New York

July 9, 1984

Dear Robert,

Came home to a lawn that had been mowed and to a garage that is now spotless. Cut flowers all over the house and, speared through one of the wild roses, a note from Michael—"What must I do to win you back?" Must have been last night's phone call that jarred him. I told him I was seeing Bea. I told him that I was not ready for him to move back. And I told him that I had cried beyond all proportion over the lightbulb incident.

Of course, I called tonight to thank him. But a very strange thing has happened. I am not really touched by today's behavior. In fact, I feel guilty that I'm *not* really moved by his actions. Could be I'm just numb. The kids were anything but indifferent to Michael's surprise—Jeanne wouldn't stop doing cartwheels and Judson *refused* to remove his new catcher's mitt at dinner. Maybe I'm just numb.

He's coming to the Emmys. I'll snap out of it by then.

Hope you are well.

Love, Kate

THE UNCERTAINTY OF THE POET (1913)
Giorgio de Chirico
Oil on canvas, 105.4 cm × 94 cm / 47 × 41½ in.
Tate Gallery (T 03977)

7/10/84

Dear M—

As you wish . . .

Alicia

Michael Hammond
300 Riverside Drive
New York, New York
10025

Pawlet, Vermont

July 14, 1984
Bastille Day!

YIKES! Bea's got you on the couch, has she?
Well, *whatever works*—

So far, so good.

Love, Robert

Kismet, Fire Island

July 15, 1984

Dear Kate,

Was in the middle of barbecueing chicken for 23 of Walter's relatives. Dropped everything, *burned every breast,* BUT IT WAS WORTH IT TO SEE YOU PICK UP THAT EMMY!!!!!!!

"SHE's MY NEIGHBOR!!!!" I yelled. "Her name is KATE and I SOLD HER HER FIRST SET OF ENCYCLOPEDIAS!"

So *congratulations!*

Afterwards I had the strangest dream. I was 16 and waitressing again. Michael came into La Parisienne, asked for chicken (*poulet chasseur*), and instead I served him a nice, light, purée of arsenic! He thanked me and I had this horrible feeling that I wouldn't see him again. I feel like a murderer even telling you this. But what I really hope is that he is well and that you two *are* back together IF that's what you want.

Will call when I get back—around August 1.

Love, Elaine (Walter, Terry, and Josh say Congratulations)

[unsent letter]

Inwood Road
Pleasantville, New York

July 17, 1984

M–

You know, very well, that it's against regulations to make love to Emmy winners. But I'm glad we came home instead of going to the party. You've rattled me, though; the next day was Bea-day:

"I'd like to get back to the point about your always taking responsibility for things."

I saw no need for Bea that day. I had fallen back in love with you.

"Does it affect your sex life?"

"Bea . . ."

"Do you feel that you are the initiator?"

I thought about Emmy night and about how one of the best things about it was that you had been passionate. Very passionate. So passionate that it seemed to me an affront to the evening to think of it as exceptional behavior on your part.

"Sometimes," I said.

"Most of the time, or sometimes?"

"I think women have more of an appetite. It's rare to find a man who really *loves* women—that feeling of being devoured."

I thought about it some more.

"He loves me, so it's never been a problem."

"So no frustration there?"

"Well. Maybe in one respect."

"What's that?"

"It occurs to me that I usually pounce first."

"The question of appetite?"

"Not really."

I knew, goddamn her, that Bea would come back with a "Why?"

"Why, then?" she asked.

"It's funny . . . I guess that by initiating . . ." I stopped. "It's hard to explain."

"Take your time."

I took a moment to calculate how much Bea gets for her time. The results made me capable of thinking faster.

"I think that what I'm doing when I initiate . . ." And suddenly it came to me. "It's like knocking on a door to see if someone's home."

Bea looked perplexed.

"To see if someone's home *emotionally*," I added.

"That's interesting," Bea said, thinking for a moment. "And is Michael home for you emotionally?"

"He always responds."

"That's not what I'm asking."

I felt very empty, bottomed out.

"Last night he was."

Bea asked what had made last night so unusual and I started to cry.

"Don't want to talk about it," I said. I apologized for *always* having these breakdowns in front of her. "Don't want to spoil it . . ."

New York City

Sunday, July 19

Dearest Michael,

I'm at the Metropolitan with Judson and Jeanne. Rainy day, which has turned the Temple of Dendur (where I am sitting) into a playground with kids trying to scale the ancient Egyptian stone. The guard, a short Italian woman, can barely speak English and, with a husky whisper, keeps saying "JEW . . . JEW!" as she points to the ground. The young Renaissance historian I've been chatting with just popped up to explain to the assembling crowd that "GIU!" means "GET DOWN!" in Italian.

We've been to the European painting galleries. Judson would not leave a room containing three canvases of bare-breasted women ("The Rape of Tamar" was his favorite). Eventually he made his way to the neighboring gallery, where Jeanne and I were. Then Jeanne started acting up. She said she felt sick. I asked if it was the tunafish we had eaten for lunch. Turns out Solario's "Solome with the Head of Saint John the Baptist" was responsible (can't blame her: it's *frighteningly* real).

So here we are at the Temple of Dendur. Judson keeps saying he wants to go back to "the room with the tits." I told him I'd buy him an ice cream instead. That's called a bribe. At Judson's age, men are more easily bribed into leaving three women behind.

Love, Kate

P.S. I'm dropping this off. We just stopped by. I wish you had been home.

300 Riverside Drive
New York City

July 21, 1984

Dear Kate,

Had a feeling Dorothy would get the invitations out early. I know you hate book parties, so I don't expect you to come. Won't be too pretentious–they tried convincing me, at the last minute, to have it at that god-awful disco that used to be a church. Over my dead body.

Love,
M.

Hunter, Stein and The Poetry Society
take pleasure in inviting you
to celebrate the publication of

GREEN PARK

by Michael Hammond

on Tuesday, September 17 at 6:30 PM
at The Poetry Society of America
15 Gramercy Park, New York

Wine will be served. Reading 7:30 PM,

RSVP: Dorothy Cross
(212) 689-5287

300 Riverside Drive
New York City

August 1, 1984

Dear Kate,

The YMCA asked me to teach a one-day poetry course for children. The only thing it succeeded in doing was to make me miss Judson and Jeanne very badly.

I asked my pint-sized poets to remember their playground rhymes. A freckled eleven year old started them off:

Miss Mary Mack
all dressed in black
with silver buttons
all down her back . . .

Her friend, a toothy tow-head of the same age, sprang up:

All the girls in France
do the hoola hoola dance . . .

By this time, the shyest boy in the group interrupted with—

I love you, I love you, I love you, Almighty,
I wish that your nightgown were next to my nightie . . .

(a blissful wickedness possessed his face).

I miss my children and my wife. Hurry up and sort things out.

Michael

Bronxville, New York

August 15, 1984

Dear Kate,

No, *I will not* attend your husband's reading of *Green Park.* Wasn't Central Park good enough for him? Oh no—he had to cross an ocean because English birds, English ducks, English trees, and English people were more deserving of poetic attention!

Now that he's back in this country, I wish him poetic impotence.

Your mother, who loves *you,*
XXMom

MUDD, WHITE

New York, New York

August 25, 1984

Dear Kate,

Thanks for helping me put together the defense. Your contributions were extraordinarily intelligent and your presence was, I hope you'll forgive me, unmercifully distracting.

In the interest of getting to know you, I hope this case drags on for years.

Fondly,
John

300 Riverside Drive
New York City

August 29, 1984

Dear Mrs. Hammond,

This is Michael's muse. Olympic Airways flew me to New York for an emergency medical evacuation. We have received calls from the New York District Muse's Office claiming that your husband, Michael, is "brain dead," dessicated, and sweltering in his Riverside apartment. A routine biopsy revealed that his heart was swollen with grief. Throughout his anesthesia, he was chanting deliriously:

Cunning and art he did not lack
but aye Kate's whistle would fetch him back.

We have doctors on Mount Helicon who specialize in poetic disorders. For a few drachmas (also payable in gold), we might be able to cure him. It would cost you less to cure him at home, where he has a better chance of recovery. I have tried the usual Inspirational Resuscitation Measures (IRMs)—Pierian spring water and bolts of all kinds, with no luck.

Let me know if you are going to take care of Michael. Otherwise I will arrange for hospitalization on Mount Helicon. Under Chapter 5, Section 23, of The Poetic Code, Muses have the right to take custody of the aforementioned client where conjugal negligence can be proved.

A reply is requested no later than September 11. The patient has a poetic function on the night of the 17th and, as his insurance carrier, we are liable if he is unable to read.

Looking forward to hearing from you at your earliest convenience,

Calliope
Chief Muse and Managing Officer
Mount Helicon, Inc.

COLUMBIA UNIVERSITY

Philosophy Hall

September 4, 1984

Michael–

Back from Block Island. Just got your invitation and look forward to hearing poems from *Green Park*. I assume it's okay to invite friends like Susan and Norman. If not, let me know.

Let's get together for our usual drinking spree.

Bill

SIDNEY SCHOENHOLTZ
TAX ATTORNEY

New York, New York

September 5, 1984

Dear Mr. Hammond.

As discussed, the IRS has no problem with your filing your taxes late. I have notified them and I have told you that there will be a penalty fee.

I would suggest that you try to get them in as soon as possible, however. And, as requested, I have *not* notified Kate of your truancy.

Sincerely,
Sidney Schoenholtz

P.S. I wouldn't worry about declaring your Tsarevich earnings.

A PERSONIFICATION OF FAME
Bernardo Strozzi (1581–1644)
National Gallery
Canvas, 42 × 59¾ ins. (1.067 × 1.517 m)

9/8/84

M—

Saw your reading listed in *The New Yorker*. Won't come if you don't want me there.

Have spent the last 2 weeks on a sailboat in the Aegean, trying to roast you out of my thoughts.

A.

Michael Hammond
300 Riverside Drive
New York, New York
10025

Inwood Road
Pleasantville, New York

September 10, 1984

Dear Robert,

Bea says I'm not giving Michael a chance. Maybe she's right. Yesterday, he tracked me down in the editing room and showed up with an armful of peonies. He excused us for a moment, took my hand, led me into my office, closed the door, turned off the lights, and put his arms around me in a way that made me feel he could not hold me close enough.

I've never seen him like this. Ever since Peter died, Michael's been almost boyish in his simple need for affection. He pulled away when he saw the roses John VanDino had sent and was not reassured when I told him they were a professional "thank you" for helping John put together the defense in the first round of litigation for "Homeless."

When I saw Bea afterwards, I told her that I was very depressed.

"Why?" she asked. "Michael's finally been acting in ways you've been asking him to act—and now you're giving up on him."

Maybe she's right. Must be that I'm angry. I've had to coach Michael all these years. I have inklings that not all men need so much prodding.

"But Michael's *doing* the right things *without* the coaching," Bea said. She mentioned the lawn, the taxes, the attention. She told me that if I gave up on him now I would have to abandon my traditional complaints against him and come up with new ones.

"Could it just be," I wondered aloud, "that it's all coming too late?" Bea looked sad. "Does that ever happen, Bea?"

"All the time," she said.

Hope you are well.

Love,
Kate

SPOT WHERE GENERALS LEE AND GRANT MET.
One of the most memorable moments in 1865. The commanding generals of the Confederate and Union armies met for conference on the old stage road.

9/11/84

Dear Michael,

Will do everything I can to be at your reading on the 17th.

Love,
Kate

P.S. Liked your vulgar Calliope.

Michael Hammond
300 Riverside Drive
New York, New York
10025

Pawlet Vermont

Sunday, September 15, 1984

Dearest Kate,

On Sundays, Margaret Potter shows up at my door at 8:30 AM. "Last chance to save your soul, Robert," she says. Today I finally went to church with her—a Calvinist affair that lasted 57 minutes (and felt like the full 60). "What did you think?" Margaret asked as we walked past the minister. "I'd rather chop wood," I said.

Or, for that matter, stare at a mountain. The leaves have just started changing up here. On the way to Margaret's religious penitentiary, I noticed that my maple tree was turning crimson. Margaret picked up a newly minted sassafras leaf, shaped like a mitten, in canary yellow!

Jane used to press autumn leaves in the books from our library. After she died, they would drop out of Churchill's volumes or, as it happened today, out of Thomas Wolfe. I was reaching for Edith Wharton, but upset Wolfe. Out came the leaf, leaving an imprint shaped like an oak leaf around the following passage:

And who can say
whatever disenchantment follows
that we ever forget magic
or that we can ever betray
on this leaden earth
the apple tree, the singing
and the gold!

Jane hated all of Wolfe except, apparently, this one passage. Thought of her when I read it. Thought of you, too. Not a bad bit of poetic crooning—hope it helps.

XX from the only man for you, Robert

P.S. Regrets about the 17th. Won't be able to make Michael's reading. Promised Margaret I'd lecture the ladies club on Baudelaire—bound to cause *un scandale!*

Inwood Road
Pleasantville, New York

September 17, 1984

Michael—

Stormed off during your reading because "The Homecoming" was too painful and *too pretty:* It had *nothing* to do with *your* homecoming.

Maybe I shouldn't have showed up. I arrived, quite chaste, with three children on two arms, only to meet every woman who has ever wanted a piece of my husband.

Dropped Stu at home. Told the kids they were having a sleepover date at Elaine's. Needed time alone.

Pulled into the driveway, ran through the basement, scraped my calf on your trunk (you never replaced the lightbulb) and, a few feet later, tripped over Jeanne's stack of books.

God put those books there. And do you know what he was saying? He was saying, "Wake up, Kate! *Wake up you idiot*—YOUR HUSBAND'S NO GOOD!" Never *was,* never *will be.* All I could do was stare at the date of your loving inscription to Susan and wonder if I was pregnant while you were fucking her!

I thought we had a chance, but there is nothing more I can do to rescue this marriage. *You're no good.* And you don't take things that *should* be taken seriously *seriously.* You're weak, which makes you capable of *stunning* mediocrity.

Alicia looks at you the same way I did when I was your student. But you've probably already discovered that for yourself.

We're not going to make it.

Kate

Inwood Road
Pleasantville, New York

September 18, 1984

Robert–

HELP! Where are you? Tried calling. No answer. Called Bea. She said we hadn't been dealt a full deck of cards.

"*We* haven't been dealt a full deck of cards!? *I* haven't been dealt a full deck of cards–*for years!*"

"You have every right to be angry."

"Every right to be angry? I have *exclusive rights* to *MURDER!*"

Complete breakdown. I ran well into someone else's hour and Bea just let it happen.

"I know Michael has his charms, Kate, but he really can be an irresponsible sonofabitch when it comes to the people he loves. It takes a certain kind of woman to put up with his pattern of behavior and my hunch is that you're not the one."

Bea's *RIGHT*. And, as with all moments of clarity, a temporary peace came over me. It was as if someone had said, "Come on in, the water's warm" and, as promised, it *was* warm. It was soothing–until 15 years of history erupted to the surface.

"Who *is* the one? Who's going to *get* him?"

"That's not the question you should be asking yourself," Bea said.

"What *SHOULD* I be asking myself?"

"You might ask yourself why *you* want him so much."

All I could do was ask Bea, "What am I going to do?" I must have repeated the question a thousand times. What *AM* I going to do? Michael calls me constantly. I just tried calling you, again. *Do you know what I'm talking about!?*

Too proud and hurt to tell you here,

Kate

300 Riverside Drive
New York City

September 20, 1984

Dearest Kate,

I'm no good, but hear me out all the same. Take my calls or let me talk to you in person.

You *know* the business with Susan is in the past. I did *not* expect her to be in London. I wanted to tell you, but the whole thing felt so distant, so aberrant and so *wrong,* I was hoping that, for your sake, you would not find out about something that would only hurt you.

There was *nothing* between us in England. Please believe me.

I must see you.

Love, Michael

45 West 89th Street
New York, New York

September 21, 1984

Dear Michael,

I'm not a homewrecker. Seeing your wife and two children was more than I could take. Your daughter looks like Kate (lucky Jeanne) and Judson looks just like you.

You don't know what will happen with your marriage. And I wouldn't want to affect the outcome in any way.

You should know that the poems were beautiful. Don't quite understand why your wife didn't stay for the best one. Judson and his friend were stretching rubberbands to the deployment stage—maybe Kate thought they would distract other listeners.

XX Alicia

P.S. I would like to remain your friend. Feel free to call me, if you want to.

Inwood Road
Pleasantville, New York

September 23, 1984

Dear Robert,

Thanks for calling. I'm a mess. And I'm sorry you're being dragged through all this. Up until the night of the reading, I had begun to see things more clearly. Now, I'm confused and hurt. Infidelity's undone all my good work. Instead of making rightful demands on Michael, any pride I have *also* says, "Make him want you"—even though this response, if appropriate at all, was only appropriate ten years ago. *Whatever* the response (because, for some reason, one *feels* the need to respond): *nothing* will alter the past, or make any current problems disappear.

Bea says that trust is a difficult thing to restore. I wonder about Alicia. Oh Robert, do you think Michael capable of having an affair with a 27-year-old student? You say that, if the business with Susan is that far in the past, I might find it in my heart to forgive Michael. But what if something is going on with his student?

All these questions, all this searching. It *embarrasses* me to be so self-involved.

Love, Kate

New York, New York

September 23, 1984

Dear Kate,

After extensive research, I have concluded that you are now FAIR GAME. I know these things take time. I won't push. I'm no poet, but I'm a good man, with a big heart and a very strong pulse.

Fondly, John

P.S. In my not-so-spare time, I have committed "She walks in beauty, like the night" to memory. Please call if you would like to hear a lawyer's reading of Byron.

[unsent letter]

Inwood Road
Pleasantville, New York
September 27, 1984

R—

Showdown on Inwood Road. A car pulled into the driveway. Judson and Jeanne rushed out like bloodhounds. I went out to see who it was. Michael was standing in the driveway. "I'm staying," he said. The bloodhounds were licking from his hand.

The Good Humor truck intervened. I sent the kids away for ice cream. "It doesn't work this way," I told Michael. "You can't just show up and expect things to be as they were."

"I love you," he said, pulling me towards him. He locked his wrists against the small of my back and took me to him. His mouth skimmed over my neck, my chin, my eyes, and landed in a hungry, inquiring way on my mouth.

"You always kiss me when you want to shut me up," I said.

He looked startled. He held me at elbow's length, his deep brown eyes looking wide and honest.

"Robert says I must ask you something."

"Ask me whatever you like."

"In the unlikely event that I ever forgive you, Robert says I must ask you something."

"Fire away," he said quietly.

Having paved the way for the question, its utterance proved more difficult than I had imagined.

"What about Alicia?" It pulled like a burr even to release the question.

"What about her?"

"Just tell me the truth," I said. I was staring at Michael's new shoes, which, unfamiliar as they were, made me realize how out of touch we had been. When I looked up, he looked very serious.

"It's over," he said. He drew his breath and was silent.

After the affair with Alicia had been confirmed, I didn't have the strength to ask any more questions. It was all I could do to listen to Michael explain that it had happened when Peter was dying. He said he had been angry with me for leaving when he needed comfort and "selfishly," he said, sought that comfort from Alicia.

I remembered all the times I had needed Michael when he had been away. There had been the ridiculous episode with Bill, but, for the most part, it had never occurred to me to turn to the nearest available source of comfort: Is *he* so weak as to move from comfort to comfort in life? Had it *ever* crossed his mind that he might be hurting me? The circumstances, it *is true*, were exceptional—but don't exceptional circumstances *test* the exceptional man? Or can it be that Michael is in love with Alicia?

"What was it about Alicia?" I asked.

"Don't start this," he said, "I've told you the truth. She's been the only one since Susan."

"What was it about her?"

"I don't understand why you do this."

"Just tell me. I have a right to know."

Michael looked very tired. "It's very simple, really," he said, quietly and deliberately, "she accepts me as I am."

I have been hearing that remark echo ever since Michael said it. Probably because it makes me think that there is no compelling reason for Michael to come home if somebody out there accepts him as he is. I had once been that person for Michael. I had once accepted him as he was.

But I have changed. I am angry with myself for changing so much and angry with Michael for *not* changing along with me. I keep thinking of Peter and Cathy as the perfect couple, growing together at the same rate—but that hadn't lasted either, for different reasons. So, Robert, what *does* last? What *will* last? Does *anything* last?

"What would Peter think?" I asked suddenly. I hadn't meant to shame Michael. But he looked ashamed. As for me, I have *never* forgiven myself for being away when Peter died.

Michael and I stood next to each other, sullen, sad, and awkward.

"Just let me come home," he said, putting his arms around me. "We'll work it out."

I wasn't sure we would. I told him I needed more time. He watched Judson and Jeanne approach, carrying their popsicles, as well as two for us.

"May I stay until you make your decision?"

I said no.

"Will you know very soon?"

I said yes.

Michael kissed the children and made his way to the car. As he was about to open the car door, he looked back and said, "Shall I send you a copy of *Green Park*?" I said yes. . . .

Fall

And the days are not full enough
And the nights are not full enough
And life slips by like a field mouse
Not shaking the grass.

Ezra Pound

Inwood Road
Pleasantville, New York

October 17, 1984

Dear Michael,

Thank you for sending *Green Park*. Your inscription, why not say it, really got to me. The poems are your best. In some of them, I recognize things. But I see where you have improved on life. Strange profession of yours that requires you to lie so beautifully.

I guess you made *us* up in your poems—especially in "The Homecoming." But, you know, all these years, I have been equally imaginative. I have been supplying our relationship with things that were really not there.

I am still trying to sort out what *is* there. I still love you (that has nothing to do with it). My making stuff up was an act of love. I just made the mistake of doing it *out here,* where things *also matter.* Sometimes I think I'm the real poet—all these years, I've tried to make it work.

Love, Kate

Inwood Road
Pleasantville, New York

November 19, 1984

Dear Mom,

Thanks for the assorted chocolates; the dark ones work best for morale. But I really don't want you to worry because I'm a great deal stronger. My concentration is coming back and I've started shooting the ballet series for Adele. After Elaine heard about the project, she said, "All those men in leotards will do you good." She knows about Michael. I've stopped being as secretive about our problems. People say things like, "*Take it from me,* it's the oldest story in the world." And I think it's their veiled way of speaking from experience.

Michael showed up today to show me the "splendid" job he had done preparing *last year's* taxes. I thought I was going to kill him. I thought I was going to kill Sidney for not telling me. But I didn't. I told myself to look at the lawn, to remember how clean the garage and the basement were. Accept him *as he is* (or let him go) I told myself. I reminded myself that Michael is an English professor and a poet—*not* a tax accountant. After all, that's what we pay Sidney to do.

And because *I* am weak, though in a vastly different way than Michael, I let him stay. That's why he came. That's why he just happened to have two suitcases full of clothes in the trunk of his car.

I know this is not the news you either expected

or wanted to hear. I write to you in part because *I* don't want to hear what I assume will be your well-reasoned, highly charged objections—maybe, I'll concede, because I value what you say; and also because there isn't a single thing you've said that I haven't already considered myself, many times over.

I will never be able to justify this next step in your eyes. But I want you to know that I am no longer completely unstitched. I told Michael we might last a week, a month, or years—I could (*would*) not promise him *anything*. He listened; and by the time I had specified my conditions, Michael looked so serious and so relieved, I knew *he* would try to make things work, even if *we* failed. "I'll go see about that lightbulb in the basement," he said. (And, however conciliatory the gesture, I confess that he might as well have shot me at dawn or run a staple through my heart, so vividly did it bring back the evening of his reading.)

As he walked towards the basement door, I was thinking that all the decisions about my marriage were now mine—because now it's Michael who is *totally* committed. And while this is reassuring to Bea, as well as to Robert (I will *never* be able to reassure you), it makes me uncomfortable. I am terrified to think that I might *not* be willing to put up with my husband. In the meantime, I am very happy for the children.

Love,
Kate